To Joanna
Beware the mus...

SERIES SILVER

SUPERB WRITING
TO FIRE THE IMAGINATION

Catherine Fisher writes, 'I live in Wales, a country that has never lost its myths. Legend and folklore underpin most of my work; I love deep forests, old stories, all the strange, dangerous territories of the imagination.'

Her first published novel, *The Conjurer's Game*, was shortlisted for the Smarties Book Prize, and *The Candle Man*, set on the eerie Gwent Levels, won the Tir Na n-Og prize. Her acclaimed fantasy series *The Snow-Walker's Son* was shortlisted for the W. H. Smith Mind Boggling Books Award.

the
Lammas
fieLd

—

catHeRINe fIsHeR

*Hodder
Children's
Books*

a division of Hodder Headline

To Lorraine

Copyright © 1999 Catherine Fisher

First published in Great Britain in 1999
by Hodder Children's Books
as part of Hodder Silver Series

The right of Catherine Fisher to be identified as the Author
of the Work has been asserted by her in accordance with the
Copyright, Designs and Patents Act 1988.

10 9 8 7 6 5 4 3 2 1

A Catalogue record for this book is available from
the British Library

ISBN 0 340 73699 2

Typeset by Avon Dataset Ltd, Bidford-on-Avon, Warks

Printed and bound in Great Britain by
Clays Ltd, St Ives plc

Hodder Children's Books
A Division of Hodder Headline
338 Euston Road
London NW1 3BH

PART ONE

The Silver Branch

ONE

Her skirt was o' the grass-green silk,
Her mantel o' the velvet fine,
At ilka tate o' her horse's mane
Hung fifty siller bells and nine.

TRAD.

Mick opened the case.

The flute lay in pieces in its blue velvet grooves, smudged with his fingerprints.

He took the mouthpiece out, breathed on it, and rubbed it angrily with the yellow duster he kept in the drawer. After a moment the silver gleamed; he saw himself reflected in it, hideously stretched, goblin-faced. The metal warmed with his heat, as if it came alive and was part of him; hastily he fitted the pieces together, till the flute was whole and shining. He had an hour at least. He'd use it, he thought grimly.

He played scales first, filling the dusty attic with them, up and down. The flute grew hot with his breath and his anger; he broke into doodles and snatches of tunes, and then, because all the words of the row were still tangled in him, a fast jig, wild and fierce, with as many extra notes as he could cram in.

The attic was muggy from the long July day, all its windows open and as he whistled into 'Star of the County Down' the motorized lawnmower started below with a

3

roar. Tom was driving home on it to his cottage. He always did when Mick's father wasn't around to see him.

Mick stopped and leaned out of a window. 'How much not to tell him?' he yelled.

The old man looked up and grinned. 'I could say the same to you! Had words again, haven't you?'

Mick looked sour. Then he said, 'Anyone in the Field yet?'

'Katie, you mean?'

'Anyone.'

'A few caravans.' The old man turned back. 'Tomorrow they'll start rolling in. Goodnight, lad.' The throttle was engaged; the roar sent all the jackdaws in the elms karking and swirling with annoyance.

'Good night,' Mick muttered to himself.

Leaning there, watching the tractor crawl away down the long gravel drive, he felt the silence slowly re-emerge like a frightened kitten. It told him how completely alone he was here. In all the attics of the great house, the garrets and servants' rooms and staircases; in all the suites of bedchambers and state rooms far below, in the Blue Chamber and the Oak Closet, in Lady Mary's Room, in the French Drawing Room, everything was dark and silent and shuttered, right down to the great dusty kitchens and cellars of barrels and spiders. The gift-shop would be eerily still and in the tea-rooms only the drying tea-towels would be stirring in the warm draughts. Outside too, all the formal gardens were twilit, their statues ghosts, their flowerbeds masses of scented shadow.

Stokesey Hall was a sleeping house, and only he was alive in it, high in this one bright window where the

4

reading lamp brought in the moths.

He was calmer now. The flute was getting cold.

He got the books out, propped them up and began to practise in earnest; the Mozart first, though it was still too hard for him; he made a mess of it, over and over, till he flung the book away in self disgust. Breathing deep, he went on. The pieces for his weekly lesson, the movement they were doing in orchestra, and then at last back in relief to the reels and folksongs, the things he loved best, the things he could play, his fingers quick and warm and easy. Most of them he knew by heart and they made him restless; they were wild, dancing reels and he wandered from attic to attic as he played them, through piles of boxes, down corridors, into the nursery room with its broken rocking-horse, where he propped himself on the saddle and slid into the slow, wailing sorrows of a lament. It was one he was making up, and it had no name yet, except that it was sad. Bitterly sad.

His own hot words came back to him; he blocked them out, fiercely, putting everything into the music, all his ambition, his deep desire. No matter what his father said he would take the music options and he would be a professional and he would be famous. For a moment he let himself dream of gigs and CDs and fast sessions in high-tech studios. The notes of the flute grew longer, more mournful. He could do it. He would. He just needed to practise, to be better. More than that, he thought fiercely. To be the best. The best ever.

He broke off suddenly and looked at his watch. Ten-thirty. They'd be finishing now. His father would be slapping the last forehand over the net and Sandy would be missing it, and laughing. She was hopeless at badminton, but she still laughed. The baby would be in the corner, asleep in the carry-cot. He wondered if anyone else took a baby to the Sports Centre. Still, it was better than him having to look after her. Sandy always wanted the baby close, that was natural. But his father was just as obsessed.

He played a soft A sharp, and a trill from G.

Then he stopped, and listened.

Far away, at the edge of his hearing, was a low thudding. Slowly he became aware of it, as if he had heard it a long while. Rhythmic, it beat like his heart, but further off, a long way off. Not in the house, he decided, but outside, and after a moment he slipped off the dappled horse, leaving it plunging, and went to the window.

This wing looked down on the East Lawn; beyond it the trees were a dark fringe against the twilight. The moon hung over them, a brilliant fingernail, and there were moths, hundreds of them; as he put his head out they brushed and crackled round the lit window where the lamp was, four rooms along.

The noise he could hear was a horse.

It was galloping fast; he couldn't see it yet but he could hear it, as if it came from somewhere incredibly distant and was taking an age to arrive — not on the gravel either, but on grass, though the great lawns stretched empty into the night.

An owl hoo-hooed from the wood. The hoof-thump strengthened, grew louder; it was a beat in the ground and in his head, and now even the cobwebs on the window were vibrating with the deep thud of it, or with his heart hammering in the stillness. And suddenly, between one beat and another he saw it come, as if it rode out of nowhere, over the surface of the lake and on to the dark grass; a white horse gleaming in the moonlight, as if it was wet. There were tiny silver bells on its harness; he could hear them chinking in the warm air, and even from here he could see there was someone on its back, dressed in pale clothes that swirled about face and shoulders.

He crouched below the sill, quickly. He was tingling, all the hairs on the backs of his hands raised.

Horse and rider paced across the lawn until they were under the window, in shadow.

'Mick.'

The voice was soft, a low calling.

'Mick!'

At first he thought it was Katie, that she'd come a day early, but it wasn't hers, it was an older voice, and it was oddly familiar to him, though he was sure he'd never heard it before.

In his hands the flute shivered, as though he trembled.

'Come down, Mick,' the voice said, quietly. 'I'm waiting for you.'

With a great effort he stood up and came forward, gripping the smooth wooden frame. 'Who are you?' he breathed.

The horse stirred, clinking. Far off a dog barked from the caravan field.

'Come down,' she whispered. 'I'll wait in the summerhouse.'

He stood there and watched her turn the horse and walk it slowly over the mothy lawns, the moonlight glinting on her. He was bewildered and puzzled and yet not afraid. He realised he was full of excitement, trembling with it, as if something glorious was happening. He turned and ran out of the room. Tossing the flute in with the books, he raced down the servants' stairs and the Great Stairs and ran along the kitchen corridor to the back door. Unbolting it he slipped through, ran over the cobbled yard and swung round on to the lawn, a smooth darkness under his feet.

The night was warm, smelling of summer. In the beds under the windows phlox and lavender released scorches of scent.

He raced up the slight slope and there was the summerhouse, a small ghostly pagoda, and the horse was outside cropping the shorn grass, its reins trailing.

As he passed it he reached out and touched the white flank; the horse snuffled and looked at him with one eye. It was hot, sweating. It had run a long way.

The woman was inside, sitting back on the bench, feet crossed at the ankle. It was dim in here, and he paused in the doorway, unsure.

It was hard to tell what age she was. Older than Sandy, he thought. Thirty? Her cropped hair was dark and glossy; the pale dress seemed green, but it changed and blurred in the shadows like leaves at midnight. She wore dangly moon earrings that glinted.

'I'm sorry,' he muttered. 'I don't know you.'

'Yes you do.' She had something in her hands, on her lap; she was fingering it. A branch, the leaves silvery. She looked up from it, eyes bright. 'You called me here.'

Bewildered, he shook his head. 'It's my father you want.

We've got the same name. He's the estate manager.'

'Not him. You, Mick.' She was smiling at him now, ruefully. She turned sideways, swung her feet up on the bench and clasped her knees over the long dress. 'I heard you playing, up there in the attic. It sounded strange, floating out over the lawns and the trees, over the lake. That was why I came. Understand?'

Behind him the horse cropped grass, with tiny tearing bites.

'No . . .'

'It was good, but it could be better. I thought you might need some help. One lesson a week's not much, is it?'

He stared at her. 'How did you know that?'

'I know.' She stood up, tall, and the branch tinkled. 'So I came. To help.'

He shook his head. 'You've come for the Fair? The Lammas Fair?'

'That too.'

'You're a musician?'

'Not exactly.'

He frowned at her, and the silver leaves and fruit stirred, a low, enticing chime.

'What is that?' he asked, fascinated.

'This?' She smiled, as if she'd been waiting for him to ask. 'This is what I've brought you.' Then she shook it, softly.

The sound came out and caught him like a sharp pain. The beauty of it was breathtaking; a subtlety of notes that chimed and seemed to go on chiming only an instant, but when it had faded he was cold and the moon had moved across the sky and the woman and her horse

9

were gone, as if they'd never been there.

Astounded, Mick stared at the empty bench.

After a while he went in and sat on it, feeling it for warmth, but there was nothing. And the grass seemed smooth, without hoofprints.

He looked at his watch. It was half past eleven. With a sudden shock he heard the car; leaping up, he saw it come smoothly up the drive and stop, and the inside light went on. There they were, his father leaning back for the cot and Sandy in her sweatshirt with the racquets, laughing, all lit up, all enclosed for a second in the glass box of the car.

The driver's door opened.

Mick got up. Keeping in the shadows, he raced back to the house.

TWO

Conle said, 'Where have you come from, woman?'
The woman replied,
'I have come from the Lands of the Living.'
ADVENTURE OF CONLE

'This is the Gilt Room.'

He threw the doors open and walked in. Behind him the group of visitors gave a murmur of amazement, as he'd known they would. The golden splendour of the room was always a surprise, even for him; it was all gold, golden mouldings and swags and cornice, the great ornate fireplace, gilt-edged panels of gods and satyrs.

'If you look up,' he said, and grinned as all their heads bent back in unison, 'you'll see the famous ceiling. Painted in 1688 by an unknown artist, it shows the sun-god Apollo, patron of music and poetry, on the mountain of Parnassus, surrounded by the nine Muses.'

Necks craned, they stared up at it, a confection of clouds and draped plump women in langourous attitudes, and just then the sun came out. Instantly the golden room took fire. On the ceiling Apollo lounged, gloriously radiant, fingering his harp. He seemed to gaze down at Mick and smile.

A scatter of music rippled through the room. For one moment Mick thought the painted fingers had moved, but then out of the window he saw a horse and cart driving up the avenue; a bright gypsy-painted contraption with Martin Frobisher driving and his son beside him, the fiddle to his chin, breaking out into a reel.

Ceiling forgotten, the visitors stared.

'Gypsies?' one woman asked, puzzled.

'Musicians, for the folk festival. The Great Lammas Fair.' Mick went over and opened the casement. 'Martin!'

He waved, and the big man waved back. 'How's tricks, lad?'

'Fine. Fine. See you later.'

The cart swung and jolted round the gravelly track. Mick watched it, seeing the cooking pans clanking from the hooks underneath. Then he pulled his head in and turned to the obedient group already drifting to the door. 'And now, if you'll follow me please, we'll go below stairs.'

When the tour was over he left the group in the Housekeeper's Shop, among the sweet-smelling soaps and jams and tea-towels with Stokesey Hall printed on them. Mary, at the till, leaned over. 'Your Dad says go for your lunch.'

'How about an ice-cream for a hard-working guide?'

She shook her head, wryly. 'All right. But don't tell anyone.'

Mick took one out of the fridge and wandered outside, biting through the thin cold chocolate. Already the day was hot, the sky blue and unclouded. He idled between the thick hedges of the Yew Walk, the sun scorching his neck, into the Cedar Garden where visitors picnicked among beds of lupins and phlox. Wasps darted into the brickwork. A small boy was having a tantrum under the arch into the Maze, ignored by his parents, who were poring over the map.

Mick ate the ice-cream slowly, licked the wooden stick and flipped it into a bin. The sun felt good after the coolness of the great rooms; he felt as if it was reaching right into him, its rays warming him back to life. He pulled his collar loose and tugged his tie off. Doing a few tours was easy enough – he knew the talk off by heart – but he hated having to dress as if he was in school.

And then instantly came into his mind the memory of the woman in the summerhouse. All morning he hadn't let himself think about her; whether she had even been real. But the chime of that branch never seemed to have left him; he was sure it had rung through his dreams all night, a single pure chord just beyond hearing. He almost thought he could catch the echo of it now, behind the breeze and wasps and people's voices, and the bursts of static from the main stage, where they were testing the sound system. Who was she? And what did she mean, that he had called her?

Abruptly he ran down the Lavender Walk and into a tiny side gate marked PRIVATE. In the house he raced up three storeys of servants' stairs, along the corridor and into his bedroom with its single huge round window.

Pulling off shirt and tie he rummaged in the drawer for his scruffiest T-shirt, the red and purple one. He pulled his jeans on and then went through to the kitchen of their flat, where Sandy sat with the baby on her knee, feeding it something from a bottle.

She smiled up at him. 'In the oven. Can you manage?'

Carefully he manoeuvred the hot dish out with a cloth.

'Have some salad with it. Oh, you beast!' She wiped the dribbled milk from Anna's chin with one finger.

'Yuk,' Mick said.

'You were like this once.'

'Never.' He piled on tomatoes.

'Have a good morning? Did you get any tips?'

'Fiver from a retired-colonel type. A few pounds from old ladies.'

She giggled. 'I'm sure you charm all the old ladies, Mick. You make sure your father pays you as well, mind.'

He frowned, eating so he wouldn't have to answer. He didn't get any money. Working on the tours paid for his flute lessons. She didn't know that – she'd have been annoyed at his father, but he felt too stubborn to tell her.

The baby made a gurgle in her throat and spluttered. Sandy patted her on the back. 'So, what are you doing this afternoon?'

'Helping at the Fair.'

She laughed. 'Of course! I'm looking forward to this famous Fair. I suppose you know all the musicians, if they come every year – they must be old friends by now.'

He nodded, swallowing. 'Some of them. The Frobishers are here, all the Irish bands, Tam Jones the piper, and the dancers from Llangollen, and, well, there are loads of others. Fiddlers, jugglers, storytellers, Morris men. You'll love it. It's a fortnight, and it's been here every year, for centuries. To celebrate the harvest.'

'Isn't there some sort of weird old ceremony?'

'The Ritual. That's on Lammas Night.' He glanced up. 'Weren't you here for it last year?'

Sandy looked coy. 'Your father hadn't brought me home yet.'

14

He shook his head, pouring orange juice. It had happened so fast. A year ago he had never even seen her, and now she was his stepmother, and he had a sister, but when Anna was ten he'd be twenty-six. They were so far apart. Different families. In fact, he was nearer Sandy's age than Anna's. It made him feel strange.

Someone walked along the corridor, the old boards creaking, and then his father came in with a file of papers that he dumped on a chair. He kissed Sandy absently and took the baby, swinging her high and making baby-talk to her as she gurgled.

'She'll be sick!' Sandy warned, getting up.

Mick cut himself a slice of cake.

His father looked over. 'Been busy?' he asked, his voice strained.

'A bit.' Mick ate the cake, not tasting it. Part of him wanted to say more, but he wouldn't. Last night's row still hung round them like a plucked note, the wrong note, distorting the air.

His father put Anna back in her cot. 'What a morning! The dancing stage slopes, there's a sump of mud blocking the caravan field where that culvert's broken, and a visitor fell down some steps in the Rose Garden.'

Sandy giggled.

'I knew you'd find that funny.'

If it had been me that laughed, Mick thought, he'd have hit the roof. He stood up. 'I'm going down to the Field.'

His father rustled the newspaper open. 'What a surprise.' Sandy frowned at him but Mick didn't care. Giving her a shrug he went out.

The Lammas Field was busy. From the car park a trail

of deep blue banners hung, each painted with a golden ear of corn. At the hedge old Tom was hammering in metal pegs for the entrance booth. 'Katie's here,' he said, looking up.

'Where?'

'Down the end. Nearest row. Looking for a job, are you?'

Mick backed off, grinning. 'Not yet.'

He wandered among the craftsmen's tents; gaudy striped awnings, blue and red and gold, saying hello to the old faces and nodding at new ones. The rich familiar smell of bruised grass came to him, and other things, redolent of summer; candlesmoke, thyme, incense sticks, some aromatic oil, frying sausages, the sweet syrupy smell of doughnuts from a stall. Hammers and banging disturbed the birdsong. Both the stages were silent now, but down at the camp someone was playing Irish pipes, and as he listened a bodhran joined in, the low rapid patter so familiar that it made him smile. For the next two weeks Stokesey would be full of music, nonstop, exciting, wonderful. That was why he loved the Fair.

The last booth in the row was barely up; from inside it came giggles. The cloth sides crumpled and then straightened again till they were taut, and then with a screech the flap opened and Katie sprawled out backwards, and stared up at him from the grass.

'Hi,' he said.

'Mick!' She tried to get up but just then the whole contraption shut up like an umbrella and collapsed, and hoots of laughter burst out from inside, the striped cloth bulging with groping hands.

16

Giggling, Katie knelt up and helped Mick find the entrance; they pulled it wide and one by one her father and mother crawled out, gasping and red-faced till the four of them sprawled on the grass round the heap, laughing helplessly.

'What on earth are you doing?' Mick managed at last.

'Putting it up, idiot!' Katie rolled over and caught her breath. She scrambled up on to her knees, still grinning. 'So how are you?'

'All right. Fine, thanks.'

She was taller, he thought, and this year she'd dyed her hair orange, and there were streaks of yellow in it, plaited tight with multicoloured threads. She wore a long blue crumpled dress, probably hand-dyed, and beads. Her feet were bare, and muddy.

She pulled a strand of hair between her fingers. 'Like it?'

'It's better than the green.'

'Oh the green! That was brilliant. I might do that again next year. You look thinner.'

Suddenly he wanted to talk to her, to tell her all about his father and Sandy and the baby, but then she knew all that — he'd sent a letter at Christmas. And her parents were talking to him, Calum pumping his hand with a huge blacksmith's fist. 'All the usuals here?'

'I'm not sure yet.'

'It'll be a good Fair.' Jean McBride lay back and looked up at the sky. 'Trust my Romany blood. A hot month, and a good harvest.'

One thin cloud crossed the sun. Mick, suddenly restless, scrambled up. 'I'll go and get some of the groundsmen to give you a hand with this.'

Calum grinned at him. 'Take your time. I'm quite happy to lie here.'

Katie came with him. Walking across the Field she said 'How's the music going?'

'Fine.'

Now he had the chance, he didn't want to talk. She flashed a quick glance at him. 'Playing tonight?'

He nodded. The Fair opened with a ceilidh, and he was playing in the band, a last-minute replacement. Probably because they couldn't get anyone else. Thinking about it made him feel glad and nervous all at once. Katie jumped a patch of nettles.

'Gone all shy on me.'

'Don't be daft.' He said it roughly, then ducked under the ropes of the beer tent and along the row of awnings.

Halfway down he stopped.

The notes jangled, clear and sharp in the breeze, and as he turned he saw they were made by wind-chimes, strange ones, small silver moons and odd jagged lightning shapes that swung and tinkled in the warm air. Above the stall the sign said ROWAN. Bunches of dried herbs hung there, making the air pungent; something was boiling in a small pot at the back. Rows of candles lined the stall, carved into faces, trees, fruit, eerie gnarled snakes, coiling and unwinding; some were burning, their tiny flames almost invisible in the sunglare. A woman was standing there, one hand against the tent prop, her red hair cropped short, tiny silver moons glinting from her ears.

'Hello again, Mick,' she said.

THREE

I will give my love an apple without e'er a core.
I will give my love a house without any door.

TRAD.

Katie came back, looking interested.

Mick didn't know what to say. 'Hello,' he muttered. His glance took in the dim, cluttered interior.

The woman smiled, as if she knew what he was looking for. She came out into the sunlight and nodded at Katie. 'I'm Rowan. An old friend of Mick's. You must be Katie McBride. He's told me all about you.'

Katie looked surprised. 'Has he? I'd love to know what.'

There was an awkward silence; Mick looked hot and embarrassed, so she reached up and jangled the wind-chimes. A cascade of soft notes tangled and hummed. 'I like these. My father makes some, but these have a stranger sound. More wistful. You didn't make them yourself, did you?'

'No.' Rowan shook her head, amused. 'I have friends who do that.'

Mick was barely listening. What did she mean, he had told her? He hadn't told her anything. He didn't even know who she was. But no. That wasn't quite true. It was as if he did know, but couldn't remember how, or from where.

'Last night,' he said, blurting it out. 'Where did you come from?' She looked at him, a warm, concerned look. 'You know. Over the hills and far away. The Land of the Young.'

The wind-chimes jangled, their odd notes chiming in Mick's head like a tangle of words, not understood but felt, as if in some unknown, eerie language. All at once he realised she was teasing him, and it annoyed him. He swung away. 'Come on,' he said abruptly to Katie, 'let's find Tom.'

She nodded, intrigued, walking out on to the sunny grass.

Rowan said quietly, 'Ready for the ceilidh tonight? Not nervous?'

A shiver of fear ran through him. 'Of course not. Why should I be?'

'You shouldn't. Not now I'm here.'

He didn't move, looking at the candles, the small flames guttering. 'That branch . . .'

'Yes.' She smiled, her eyes green as glass. 'I know. You can still hear it, can't you?'

'No . . . not really.'

'You can. You'll always hear it now. So don't worry about the ceilidh.' She turned and went to the back of the stall. For a second he stayed, oddly happy.

Then he walked after Katie.

When the McBride's stand was finally up, and Calum was unpacking the forge and some tall iron candlesticks, Mick lay sprawled in the grass looking up at the sky, feeling the sweat cool on his chest. Beside him, Katie

threaded daisies together, splitting the stems carefully
with a long fingernail.

'So, come on,' she said suddenly. 'Who is she?'

'Who?'

'That woman. Rowan. What have you told her about
me?'

'Nothing.'

She looked up. 'Not the impression I got!'

'I don't know who she is. She just turned up.' He
rolled over, rubbing grass from his hair. Around them
the Field was quiet; an afternoon hush, all the stalls
half-ready or shuttered, their striped awnings hanging
in the heat, the banners unmoving. The air seemed
ominous with silence; over the trees the gables of the
Hall rippled as if everything waited for tonight, for the
Fair to begin.

Katie had stopped threading, and was watching him.
'You're nervous.'

'A bit.'

She grinned, the orange sweep of hair falling in her
eyes. 'Well there's no need to be. No one's going to tell
you off if you get it wrong.'

'This is different.' He hugged his knees, tense. Then he
said 'Last night, I told Dad I want to be a musician. Go to
college to study music, I mean. And then be freelance –
do recordings and CDs and go round the festivals and
play; get into a band.'

She nodded, wiping her hands in her dress. 'I'll bet he
loved that.'

The birdsong from the wood was muted. Mick said,
'We yelled at each other. He went on and on about
getting a real job, about money. It's always money. I

21

couldn't explain. I never can. I just get choked up.'

'What about Sandy?'

'Oh, she keeps out of it.' Mick pulled a stem out of the grass and bit it, absently. 'She's all right, but he's so . . . straight-laced. As if he's tied himself up tight and can't get free. And he just won't listen!'

'You'll have to talk him round. Get him used to the idea.'

He snorted. 'Fat chance. And it's worse than that. He kept saying I'd never be good enough. That I didn't have any real talent. That I'd end up a failure in some squat without any money.'

'At least you'd have tried.'

'Maybe.' He stood up, blocking the sunlight. 'I'd better go and put in some last minute practise. See you later.'

Katie wound the daisy chain carefully round her neck. 'Don't get worked up. I know you, you will. He's got all summer to come round.'

Nodding, he turned and walked hurriedly over the Field. It was all right for Katie. Her parents would let her do anything; they knew about being free, about doing what you had to. They'd back her. Nobody backed him. But as he walked faster, between the corn banners and over the gravel of the car park, he knew he hadn't told her the worst of it, had barely admitted it to himself, the terrible gnawing doubt that maybe his father was right: that he wasn't good enough, and never would be. That was what scared him.

There was no one in the flat. He took an apple from the bowl and the flute and tin whistles from his room, glancing a moment out of the window at the tourist coaches going home in a long line down the drive. The Hall was busy, making lots of money. That should please his father, he thought bitterly.

Downstairs he met Sandy struggling to get the pushchair in the side door, and held the baby for her. Anna was asleep; warm from the sun and surprisingly heavy.

'Going out?' Sandy said. 'What about tea?'

'I don't want any. I need to practise.'

She pulled his hair playfully and took the baby back. 'First night nerves. I'd come, but there's no babysitter. Your Dad will.'

'He won't,' he said. 'He's never come to anything yet.'

Outside, the lawns were empty; a few fragments of litter lay on the smooth grass. He ran down the Yew Walk and up into the woods, all the rooks karking high in the trees overhead. Few visitors came here, especially now, towards evening; the wide shaven walks were lit by slants of late sunlight. At the end of one a pheasant stood, staring at him stupidly.

This was his own private route; he pushed through the undergrowth to a tangle of hazel hedge. In one corner he had forced a hole wide enough to squirm through, scratching his arms. He came out into dazzling sunlight, and the cornfield.

It was huge, stretching far, and the crop was ripe and golden, swaying in the warm air, a faint endless rustling louder here than the distant purr of cars. There was a small trail into it, narrow and winding, and as he followed it the spiky husks were chest-high around him. Underfoot the soil was chalky and dry, baked into hard ridges.

Deep in the crop the path ended in a tiny clearing, barely big enough for him to sit down, the stiff golden stalks hiding him completely, high above his head. Knees drawn up, he felt the warmth of the earth, seeing nothing but a circle of blue sky. He often practised here. No one could see him or bother him. Best of all, no one could hear his mistakes. When he'd first started playing, his father had groaned every time the flute came out.

He ran through everything, his fingers stubbing on the wrong stops too often, so that he stopped and swore and started all over again, the pit of his stomach cold with worry. They'd all be there, hundreds of people, and the band were all used to that, all except him. Had they really wanted him, he wondered? Maybe Huw had only been desperate when he asked. And yet the Fair was full of musicians. Angrily he speeded up the jig, feeling it cheer him, put life in him, but whenever he stopped the endless rustle of the corn brought back his desperation.

It was colder now; the sky had clouded. A small ripple of movement swished the crop, a shiver around him and through him, so that he lowered the flute uneasily and knelt up, looking out over the darkening field.

The sun was low; great clouds devoured it. As he watched, it slipped away. It was later than he'd thought; he had to get to the sound check. But still he didn't move. In the silence the field breathed and stirred. A heron flapped heavily over the hedges.

Turning his head, Mick looked back at the wood.

It had changed.

He knew that, instantly, though he couldn't say how. The trees were dark, the early moon pale and nebulous through their branches. He'd known them all his life, but now they were different, as if the twilight had wizened them, contorted their branches into unnatural shadows. Mist drifted among them; sometimes he saw it clearly, but then it seemed to turn sideways and slink out of his vision. In the time between day and night something had happened to the wood.

He scrambled up, the flute icy in his hands.

The corn rustled. There was no way through it; he'd have to go back through the trees and he'd have to go now, or he'd be late. He crammed the whistles into his pocket, stiff against his leg.

Walking through the corn, uneasiness rose in him. The wood was tense, rustling with small movements. He hurried, but when he came to the hole in the hedge he crouched, looking through it with something like dread. It wasn't the same. It was a pit, a tunnel, worming into the dark.

Mick closed his eyes. Sweat was cold on his back. This was stupid. This was just nerves.

He crawled back through, hands in the mud.

Tiny spiteful thorns caught at his sleeves.

In the wood it was worse. He walked fast, stumbling. Mist drifted in the thickets; in the corners of his eyes it contorted into faces, grotesque and beautiful, fleeting, inhuman. Something laughed, like a cat's yowl. Branches tripped him; the wood had warped; he found he was breathless and disoriented, not even sure where he was, the pale moonlight blurring on things that scuttled and twisted and perhaps weren't even there.

He leaned his hand on an ivy-covered oak; dizzy, unable to stop shaking.

Then, near him somewhere, a light piping began,

remote and high above; glancing up he saw the branches were black and crooked with outlines that squatted among the leaves. One of them slid down the trunk, head first, whispering at him.

Mick ran. He plunged down the paths recklessly, the flute in his hand flashing silver. He ran till he burst out on to the lawn, and almost crashed into the woman who was sitting there.

He stopped dead, foolish, skin crawling with tension.

Rowan stood up. 'There you are. I've been waiting.'

She came closer and looked over his shoulder, into the dark. 'Are they bothering you? You'll get used to them, Mick.'

She turned him round, as if he'd been a little child and, catching his arm, led him over the dim lawns. 'Come on now. You can't be late, tonight of all nights.'

He shook his head, bewildered. 'What were they? Those shapes?'

She laughed. 'Every queen must have her court. Think of them as your new family. But you should concentrate on the music now. Tonight is the start of it, Mick. You'll see.'

Before them the Lammas Field was lit with lamps and candles and strings of brilliant light-bulbs. Music rang out from the main marquee; the Field thronged with people.

He stopped. 'I'm not sure I can do it,' he muttered.

Her nails were sharp on his skin, her eyes green and narrow as she smiled back at him. 'You can now,' she said. 'Because we've given you the gift.'

FOUR

Weeping and treachery are unknown in the pleasant
familiar land;
there is no harsh fierce sound there, but sweet music
striking the ear.

VOYAGE OF BRAN

He leaned on the Gilt Room windowsill, head hung low, hands hot in the sun.

Even now, he couldn't believe what he had done, how he'd felt. All night he'd lain awake, dazed and happy; been silent at breakfast, spent the morning mumbling the familiar repetition of the tour, barely even seeing the visitors.

Last night still burned in him. The ceilidh had been wild, a delirium of turfsmoke and sizzling sausages and music, music that had surged up in him from nowhere, music he hadn't known he could play, his fingers fast and confident, and Huw grinning at him and improvising and Katie clapping from the dancefloor and getting whirled away shrieking by her father; all rhythmic and tangled in his head like a set of reels. He had played like someone else, hardly eating and drinking in the intervals, too taut and joyful, and terrified it would all go away.

Now he took a long breath and looked up, out at the strolling couples eating ice-cream, and a juggler tossing coloured balls in the Rose garden.

Had that been him? How could it have been? He'd never been able to play like that. Where had the confidence come from, the skill? What had she done to him?

Rowan had been there, watching, among the blue and green lights, sometimes sitting on the straw bales, sometimes dancing, always vivid, easily seen. Once he'd caught her look; it was sharp, strangely hungry, but she'd smiled and waved and he'd forgotten it. But how could it be her? The music was in him. He knew now it always had been.

'Michael?'

His father was standing in the doorway, a clipboard under one arm. Mick drew himself up, wondering how long he'd been there.

'Heard it went well last night.' Mr Carter came in; the door slid shut. Around them the gold panels blazed in the sunlight.

'Yes . . . I think so.'

'Sandy says you were good. Quite inspired, in fact.'

There was a dry edge to his voice; Mick heard it and his dream went sour. 'You should have been there,' he muttered.

'Oh, Sandy wanted to go, and someone had to babysit. Besides, I have quite enough of the Fair all day. You don't know all the paperwork that goes on to run this annual nuisance. Someone has to do it.'

He had crossed to the fireplace and was crouched, looking up into the chimney. Straightening, he made a few notes.

Mick watched him. They were alike — so everyone said. He wondered if his hair would be that thin, when he was forty. That wasn't old. His father always seemed older, except when he was with Sandy. Always firm and clear, and never doubting himself. Always right. He was looking up now.

'Haven't you got any more tours?'

'One.'

'Well they'll be waiting. Remember not to take them into Lady Olga's Room – the carpet's still not dry after the leak and I've just asked Jennifer to take all the china out and clean it. And for heaven's sake watch out for kids with chewing gum.'

He nodded, hopelessly, but when he was half-way to the door his father said suddenly, 'And Sandy says ask Katie for tea.'

Mick stared back, but his father was writing again. All around them the room shone; Apollo lounging on his clouds, smiling down at them sadly.

Katie could always manage to juggle three balls easily; it was the extra one that fooled her. She grabbed too far for it, and suddenly they were all in the wrong places, and then in the grass. She kicked them, annoyed. From the back of the stand the clang of the forge sounded; idly she wandered among the candlesticks and cast-iron sculptures, straightening one, rubbing dust off another. Then she went and sprawled on a rug at the front, looking out.

On its first day, the Fair was busy. On the far stage a group of Appalachian dancers were lost behind a crowd, their pounding clogs and claps underbeating every other sound, until it stopped suddenly in a spatter of applause. In the main marquee a fiddlers' workshop was squealing and stopping and breaking out into improvised sessions, and far down by the storytellers tent a girl was singing a clear ballad – Katie recognised it as *The Foggy Dew*. All the stalls were open, and the smell of trodden grass made her grin.

She loved this Fair. They went to many, but the Lammas Field was different; ancient and unchanging, a small world of its own, far from home, a gathering of people who came from all over the country, for the old songs and dances and customs, for the Ritual, regular as the harvest, full of old friends. It made all the dull terms in school fade into oblivion – that world where she had brown hair and a uniform and lived just like anyone else. Well, almost. But this was real: the music, the travelling, the rain drumming at nights on the caravan roof. She loved it. She'd always be here.

'I suppose you're not the blacksmith?'

Someone stood against the sun, a blurred outline. Katie scrambled up, startled. 'It's my father.'

The man nodded, wryly. 'Will he fix this?' He held out a small metal peg, badly bent. From a harp, she guessed.

'You'd better ask him. He's round the back.'

The stranger was thin; his blue shirt worn and faded with age, his longish hair fair and lank. He had a delicate, unhealthy look, as if after some long illness. Interested, Katie followed him round.

Her father was looking at the peg. 'Never straighten it. I'll make you another one. Just as good.'

'How much?'

'A quid. Just for the metal.'

The man nodded. 'Thanks.'

'No problem. It's Alex, isn't it? We haven't seen you since Priddy. Three years ago.'

30

'Four.' The harper turned, looking out at the Field. 'I've been out of things for a bit.'

He was younger than she'd thought.

'How long will it take?' he asked.

Calum shrugged. 'Say tomorrow? In the morning.'

Alex nodded, but he didn't move. Instead Katie sensed him stiffen, just a fraction; a strange tension froze his gaze. Following his look, she saw Rowan.

The woman was crossing the Field, her blue dress dark in the sunlight; she was talking to a tall thin dancer in bizarre clothes, purple and yellow and green, all patchwork, a horned headdress under his arm. Her face was sharp and amused; she ran a few steps and turned, walking backwards, her hands shaping a circle as she talked. The dancer grinned, wickedly.

'Do you know her?' Katie asked quietly.

The harper glanced at her. For a moment she glimpsed a wretchedness, a hopelessness terrible to guess at; then he looked away.

'For a moment I thought so,' he said. 'But it couldn't be.'

Chilled, Katie said 'Her name's Rowan.'

He shrugged. 'The one I knew had many names. None of them true.'

He walked off then, behind the awnings and the crowd at the food stalls, out of sight.

Katie chewed an end of orange hair, intrigued. She turned quickly. 'Who's he?'

'Alex. Forget his other name. Brilliant musician.' But two women were looking at the sculptures, and he went over to them hastily.

★　★　★

31

Mick came into the Field at about two. The Fair was crowded, and already the sun was almost too hot to bear. He bought a can of orange and drank it, watching a troupe of tiny men turn somersaults and build complex pyramids with their bodies on the trampled grass. One of them capered with a whistle, grinning evilly.

Mick tossed the can in a bin and looked over. Rowan's stall was quiet; a few people browsed there. Even from here he could smell the peculiar rank mixture of herbs and candles and incense. He went across.

His heart was hammering and his palms were hot, and he still hadn't decided what to say, what to ask, but when she came out and waved at him he knew it didn't matter.

'Come inside,' she whispered.

At the back was a screen, hung with beads and scarves. Behind that he found almost a small room, with strange low chairs and a wooden table, and a great mirror propped against the canvas wall.

'Where's your van?' he asked, curious.

'I didn't come in a van. I came on horseback, remember?' She sat down, propped her feet on the table and said 'How did it feel then, to play like that?'

He shook his head, hopeless. 'How do you know about me? Is it you making all this happen?'

The wind–chimes jangled. She smiled, her green eyes dark. 'It's exciting, isn't it? You feel full of power. It can always be like that now, if you want.'

'Of course I do,' he muttered 'but . . .'

'They call it inspiration, don't they, artists and poets?' She swung her feet down, stood up and came closer. 'None of them know what it is though, or where it comes from. But how they hunger for it! And when it comes, you have to do anything to keep it. No matter what it costs you.'

He clenched his fingers. 'What will it cost me?'

'Nothing.' She touched his hair. 'Yet.'

Stepping back, his skin cold, he said, 'But how long will it last?'

'As long as you want. You'll play better than you ever dreamed. You'll be brilliant. Everyone, even your father will say that.' She turned suddenly and went over to the mirror, reaching up. For a second Mick was quite sure nothing hung there, but as her hand came down he saw she held a wind-chime; long tiny cylinders of shiny silver, each with a star dangling from the end. She rippled it, and a scatter of pure notes rang out. She pushed it into his hand. 'The first one is a gift,' she said archly. 'But only the first.'

He found Katie at the pancake stand, squeezing syrup over something hot and sticky.

'You would,' he muttered. 'I came to ask you to tea.'

'Oh good. I'll still come.' She took a bite and grinned, pulling the other end off and holding it out to him. They chewed in silence for a moment, then Katie licked her thumb and fingers. 'Want to meet Sandy properly. And your sister.'

'Half-sister.' It still sounded strange. As he turned, the wind-chime in his pocket gave a soft clink; she said, 'What's that?'

Before he could answer someone called him. Tom came shouldering through the crowd, looking hot and bothered, his collar open. 'Mick, lad. Have you seen your father?'

33

'Not for hours. He's probably at the Hall.'

'Blast.' The old man glanced round. 'Do me a favour. Get up there and find him.'

'Why? What's wrong?'

Tom wiped his face and neck with a dirty handkerchief.

'Problem. More than that. Trouble.'

FIVE

The wind that shakes the Barley.

TRAD. REEL

'A crop circle?' Michael Carter stared round the car park in astonishment. 'Is this a joke?'

'No joke.' Tom wiped sweat from his hands.

'But that's ridiculous. You mean someone's flattened the barley?'

'In Master's field. A circle. Perfect. About eighteen feet across.' The old man shrugged. 'Every stalk lying flat.'

'My God, that's all I need!' Mick's father pushed past him, weaving angrily through the parked cars. 'Show me, quick. And let's hope no one else has seen it.'

With Mick and Katie racing ahead, they hurried across the lawns. 'Slow down,' Tom breathed. 'I'm too old to be chasing about in the heat. This way's best.'

He turned into the Yew Walk. Katie grinned at Mick. 'Sounds weird.'

He looked up, absently. 'I suppose so.'

'I forgot to tell you. Martin Frobisher said you were the best thing on the stage last night. Said you were brilliant.'

She'd thought that would delight him, but to her surprise he looked almost scared. 'That was kind of him.'

'Listen to you! Think you're a maestro already!'

'I can be better, that's all. I will be.'

They didn't go into the wood, to Mick's relief, but through the field-gate, Tom clanging it shut behind him. 'This way.'

The crop whispered and rustled; carefully they trod the sparse remnants at its edge, feet slipping on the hard furrows. Mick was uneasy; they were coming down to his practise place; just ahead he could see the familiar trail. To his dismay Tom led them down it.

'This looks like the way they got in. And here's the damage.'

The circle was uncanny. A swirl of flattened crop, each stalk lying precisely in its place, smooth and still.

Katie crouched down. 'It's amazing! I've never seen one before.'

Above her Mick stood chilled, as if the sun had lost its warmth. This had been his practise place. What had happened to it?

His father swore. 'How the hell did they do it?'

'Who?' Katie asked mischievously. 'The little people?'

'Someone from the Fair. These things are hoaxes, Katie, and someone's looking for cheap publicity.' Angrily, he scuffed at the furrows. 'What a waste! How are we supposed to harvest this!'

He turned on them. 'Listen, I don't want anyone else knowing about this, or the rest of the corn will get trampled to bits, and we'll have every weirdo in the county here. No one, mind. Katie?'

She nodded, reluctant, but Tom shrugged, looking back into the wood. 'That's no use, boss. Whoever made it knows. And they won't keep quiet.'

He was right.

By tea-time the news was all around the Field. In her cramped room in the caravan, changing into clean jeans, Katie thought about it. If it was for publicity they'd got it. And yet — who really knew how those things were made? There had been something unnatural about it, the perfection of its shape, the neatness of the flattened corn, as if some whirlwind had hovered there, or some energy gathered and hummed. She pulled a comb through the orange tangle and winced.

Later, crossing the Field, around her the Fair was closing. Fires burned in the camping field and the awnings of the stalls hung still. This was the quiet time, when the afternoon visitors had gone and before the nightly music sessions began. The time when the Fair turned in on itself. She walked down the rows of stalls where people pottered, cooking, hammering, the odd radio playing softly. Rowan's stall was empty, the hanging moons chiming.

But before she went out at the entrance, between the long banners of blue and gold, something made Katie pause, and look back.

Long shadows stretched over the grass; the smell of woodsmoke drifted. For a second she waited there, trying to pin down some nagging unease that wouldn't come. But everything seemed normal. Far down among the quiet rows of stalls someone was laughing, a sly giggle.

'You sit here.' Sandy pulled out a chair for her, then hurried round the table to where the baby crawled on a tartan blanket, picking at the fringe with sticky hands.

'She's lovely,' Katie said.

'She's a terror. Mick thinks so. Don't you, Mick?'

He shrugged, glancing at Katie quizzically.

'You're quiet,' she said, helping herself to sandwiches.

'Am I?'

'Have been all day.'

He just smiled, looking out at the sky.

They were sitting in the only private garden the flat had, high up on the roof. All around them the leads and gables of Stokesey Hall rose into intricate ridges and valleys; huge Elizabethan chimneys sprouted in clusters, their pale terracotta columns adorned with chevrons and crenelations.

Sandy had dragged a metal table and some chairs up here, and all around it were pots of geraniums and strawberries, a garden of climbers up trellises, crammed with greenery.

'I sunbathe up here,' she said to Katie, handing over a plate of cake. 'It's the only place you're sure no tourist with a camera is going to trip over you.'

'Topless?'

'If I lock the door.'

Katie giggled. Mick looked embarrassed.

'Though there are other doors. The place is a warren of rooms and stairs — it took me ages to learn my way round it. I still end up miles away in some scullery. It's an adventure just getting to the car.'

Katie liked her. She knew Mick did too, but when his father came up later, she felt the faint resentment between them like a charge. Mr Carter looked hot and harrassed. 'The local paper's been on the phone. Is it true we've had a mysterious crop circle on the estate? Can they send a photographer over?' He slapped butter on a scone ferociously. 'Didn't take them long, did it.'

'What did you say?' Sandy asked.

'Yes. No choice. At least I can keep an eye on them. Otherwise they'd just come anyway, I should think.'

'Dad says it'll be good for business,' Katie said thoughtfully.

'I dare say. But it's a pain all the same. It'll attract every nutcase in the area. Not that most of them aren't here already.'

Sandy giggled. Katie twirled an orange lock between her fingers and looked innocent.

By the time Sandy went to put the baby to bed the twilight was gathering, moths crackling and wisping over the warm leads. Mr Carter gathered plates on to a tray and carried them down. Katie came and leaned next to Mick, on a parapet that looked as though it might crumble away under her.

'Is this safe?'

He looked at it. 'Probably.'

'I just ask because I've never been to tea on a roof before.'

Mick grinned. 'And you thought your family were the odd ones.'

'It must be fantastic living here.' She gazed out over the estate. 'All these rooms and attics. All these woods.'

'All these tourists. And it's miles from anywhere. No one my age. No music, no way of getting to concerts. It's not that great.'

She frowned, kicking the stone. 'Try living in some cramped house on a council estate like some people do. You don't know you're born, Mick.'

Far below them the smooth lawns were murky now,

softening into shades of grey, the distant lake glinting under the moon. All the woods of the surrounding countryside whispered in black, rustling expanses, and beyond them, for miles, the cornfields stretched, dull and dark now, but in the daylight a sea of golden stirring harvest, the house moored like a great ark in the centre. From the Field, out of sight round the corner of the gables, faint music drifted; the wail of Northumbrian pipes, eerie and thin, as if they were lost ghost-voices, crying to be let back into the world.

'What's that?' Katie said.

She was pointing down, near the East lawn and the Herb garden.

'What?'

'That. There, Mick.'

He saw them. Small, blue lights. They bobbed, oddly, among the shrubs.

'People with lights,' he muttered.

'I don't think so.' Intrigued, she edged along the parapet.

Mick felt cold. Last night, it had been about this time, this twilight time, when the wood had changed.

'Come and see!'

He moved after her, reluctant.

The lights crackled, moving strangely, drifting, abruptly disappearing and appearing again, further off. It was hard to see what they were; sometimes they seemed like globes, then points of blue flame.

She caught his arm. 'Let's go down!'

For a moment he hesitated. Then he said, 'All right. This way.'

In the twilight they ran over the roof to a small door in a turret; Mick yanked it open, and they clattered down a tiny spiral stairway into darkness, floor after floor. At the bottom was a corridor, carpeted, the walls panelled an old brown oak. Catching him up she whispered, 'What about the alarms? Won't we set them off?'

He turned a corner. 'Don't tell anyone, but there aren't that many.'

They ran through a dim series of sculleries, pantries and larders, through the Servants' Hall where the pale moonlight lit high arched windows, and then down a dark passage under rows of coiled bells marked with the names of rooms; Katie stared up at them in fascination. But Mick was unbolting the back door; once they'd slipped through he slammed it, and jabbed a few buttons on a panel at the side.

They ran round the side of the house, over the lawns.

'There!' Katie stopped, amazed.

Alone in the darkness, the blue lights hovered. An eerie gloom drifted with them; they rose high off the ground and then sank into the grass, moving in and out of each other, a random swarm with no pattern.

Suddenly chilled, she stepped back. 'I don't think we should go too near them.'

He nodded, a dark shape next to her.

The lights hissed. They were impossible to count, winking out, swelling and fading, sometimes like flames, or stars, or bubbles.

'I think they can feel us,' she muttered.

'Don't be daft.'

'Look at them, Mick.'

The earth-lights had grown agitated, grouping closer,

swirling faster. Then with a sudden terrifying burst they erupted outwards, hurtling like streaks into Katie's face so that she screamed, feeling pain crackle all over her, tingling her hair and skin.

'Mick!' she screamed, but he was lost in sparks and shadows, and as she beat the lights away she almost thought they flickered into faces, leering and grotesque. She grabbed at him, the shock making her skin burn with an explosion of blue light that seared her palms, so she huddled and clutched them in the snapping electric sting until a voice called 'leave them!', a woman's voice, hard and commanding, and instantly, all the lights went out.

In the sudden dark she was sore and breathless; beside her, Mick picked himself up from the grass.

A single cloud drifted over the moon.

Around them, all the lawns were empty.

SIX

He went away from me
and he moved through the Fair.
Slowly I watched him
move here and move there.

TRAD.

'They sound like earth-lights to me.'

Katie spread all her fingers round the brown mug of hot tea. 'And what are they?'

Martin Frobisher stretched his legs out. His beard was thick and dark; a soft hat with a feather in shoved back on his straggly hair. He took a mug from Katie's mother, Jean. 'No-one really knows. Some say ball lightning. Others, some sort of electro-magnetic energy. Others, the faery folk.'

Katie grinned and he saw her.

'Don't mock what you don't know, Katie,' he said gravely.

From the top step she put a bare toe down and traced a swathe in the wet grass. The dew was icy, rolling in drops across her foot. 'But other people have seen them?'

'So they say.' He drank, looking round at the early-morning Field.

'Might they not have some link with the crop circle?' Katie's mother asked, stirring honey.

'Now that's possible. Carter thinks the circle's a fraud

– well, it's more than likely.' Martin sipped his tea, thoughtfully. 'I've seen plenty that were – all around Avebury last year. One at Stonehenge. But this wasn't really like those. It had something odd about it. It's so small and plain. And it tingles.'

'Tingles?' Jean asked.

'Ay. It tingles, Jean, and that's the nearest I can get to what I mean.'

They both laughed. Katie turned to tip the dregs out of her mug. 'Oh, hello!' she said, startled.

Alex was standing at the side of the stall, listening to them. In the early sunlight he looked tired, his old rust-coloured jumper frayed at the neck. 'Sorry,' he said. 'I surprised you.'

'I didn't hear you come.'

Calum looked over from lighting the forge. 'I'll be with you now, Alex.'

The harper glanced round, restlessly. 'I could come back . . .'

'No. Won't be a tick.'

'Have some tea.' Katie poured it for him and held it out. He took it, reluctantly.

'Sugar?'

'No thanks.'

Martin Frobisher was watching over the brim of his mug. 'So how are you, lad? I heard you were back.'

Alex cradled his mug with long hands. 'I'm fine,' he said sharply.

'You've got a session today?'

'Two o'clock.' He looked over. 'If the repair's done.'

'Oh it's done, all right.' Calum straightened, wiping filthy hands. 'I'll just have to find it, that's all.'

The harper frowned, and looked away. Was it her imagination, Katie thought, or did he seem disappointed? She put both feet in the dew without noticing.

Her father went into the stall; they heard the clatter and rattle of a workbox emptying. In the uneasy silence Katie pulled her hands inside the sleeves of her multi-coloured jumper and shivered. It was barely eight, and the sun was just clearing the misty woods. As she watched, the pale light touched the Field, stretching long shadows behind the stalls and banners and tents. Alex watched it too; she noticed how he stepped into the warmth, as if he was cold.

Her father came out with the peg. 'Any good?'

The harper turned it in long fingers, almost too long, she thought, as if years of plucking the strings had changed them. 'It's fine,' he said darkly. He took a pound coin from his pocket and held it out.

'Oh, forget that.' Calum squeezed his bulk on to the steps. 'Not between craftsmen. I'll come and listen to you play – from what I've heard that should be payment enough.'

Alex nodded, unhappily. 'Let's hope so.' He gave the half-full mug back to Katie. 'Thanks for the tea.'

Watching him go, Martin said, 'He's still not right.'

'What was wrong with him?' Katie asked, curious.

Martin shrugged, glancing at her father.

'Some illness,' Calum muttered. 'It's over now.'

She saw them exchange a look; it annoyed her. She turned and watched Alex walking between the tents.

'He was a great player.' Martin drank the last of his cold tea. 'I mean the best. I'd never heard anything like him. Not just the Celtic harp mind, but pipes and fiddle

45

too.' He shrugged. 'To be honest, I'm surprised to see him back. But if he's playing I'll be there, if only to give the lad some support. That sort of thing could happen to any of us.'

Katie scratched her heel. She knew if she asked again they still wouldn't tell her. But she'd find out.

All morning she was busy at the stall, and she guessed Mick was working. But by two o'clock there was still no sign of him, so she went down to the small sessions marquee on her own, leaving her mother gossiping with two other women round a dented cauldron, like the witches in Macbeth.

Putting her head in through the flap she saw that the tent was almost full. People sat on benches or on rugs at the sides, and on the central patch of grass stood a small harp and a collection of other instruments. The mikes were up, someone tapping them anxiously, a sharp crack that cut across the murmured conversation.

She went back out to look for her father. Instead, she saw Alex.

He was standing at the edge of the Field, deep among the trees there, bent over away from her. Straightening, he wiped his mouth with a handkerchief, one hand flat against the oak trunk. Alarmed, she ran over.

'Are you all right?'

He glared at her once, then away, his face white as paper.

'Can I get someone? Are you ill?'

To her alarm he didn't answer, but turned and walked deeper into the trees. She stumbled after him. 'Where are you going? They're all waiting for you.'

46

'I know they are.' He stopped and stood with his back against a tree, then squatted down on the roots, head down, hands hanging limp. Gnats danced above him in the hot air.

She bit her lip. 'I could get someone . . .'

'I don't think I can do it.' He looked up at her then, and she saw his hair was dark with sweat; his hands were clammy with it, and as he clutched them into fists they trembled.

Katie didn't know what to say. She looked round desperately for her father, or Martin, but there was no one near. From the tent a bodhran rattled impatiently, softly.

'But you're brilliant. Everyone says so.'

'I'm terrified.' He stared grimly into the trees. 'That's what it is.'

Slowly she crouched down and sat next to him. The soft crumble of wet soil moved under her fingers.

In the silence she said 'My name's Katie.'

'I know.' There was a small metal disc on a chain round his neck; both his hands came up and caught it, fingering the smooth circle over and over. 'It's ridiculous,' he whispered. 'I've played for crowds, in concert halls, pubs, studios . . . Look at me now. This is fear, Katie, this is how it feels. Everything else is gone.'

He sounded furious with scorn and shame.

She tried again. 'It's not really that bad is it? You must be used to people listening. Once the music starts . . .'

'. . . I'll be all right?' He glanced at her bitterly. 'That's what scares me, the music. Whether it will even be there.'

'You said you've done it before.'

'Before was different!' He put his forehead against his

palms, closing his eyes. 'I was different! Since then I've been in Hell. In deep, dark places . . . This is the first time I've played in public since. And I don't know if I'm good any more. She may have taken that away.'

'She?'

'Someone I knew.' He opened his eyes; they were dark and distant. 'Thought I knew.'

Worried now, Katie turned back and watched the marquee. If only someone would come out. They must be wondering where he was by now.

'Look,' she said, kneeling up. 'This is important. If you don't go in there and face it, you may never play anywhere again. At least you'll have tried. You'll feel better. I want you to do it; I really think you can, and that you owe it to all of them in there, waiting. They're not going to judge you, they just want to hear you, that's all.'

He almost smiled. 'Everyone judges you, Katie. Especially now. "Not like he used to be; they'll say. Not quite got it back, has he?" And they'll smile and feel sorry and a little bit pleased.'

She bit her lip, thinking of Martin. 'Once the music starts you'll forget them. You won't care. Look at Mick.'

'Mick?'

'A friend of mine. He played the flute at the ceilidh on Friday. He was scared stiff but he did so much better than he'd thought. You musicians, you're all nerves.'

Despite himself he smiled, tangling his fingers. 'You're a generous girl, Katie. It's not your problem.'

'My father says we stick together, the Fair people.'

For a second he was still, as if drawing on something deep in himself, so deep it took him an age to find it; then, abruptly, he stood up.

So did she. 'Are you OK?'

He was white, reckless, his pale hair dark with sweat.

'Just watch me,' he whispered.

As she slid on to the bench at the back her father squeezed up to make room. 'Thought you wouldn't make it.'

The ripple of the harp tuning up stopped her answer.

Alex sat down. He looked, just once, round the rows of faces. 'Thanks for coming,' he said, his mouth taut with tension.

With a nod to the fiddler, he started to play.

At first he was shaky, even she could tell that, but as the music gathered, the rhythm filling the warm space, he grew stronger, seemed to forget the watching faces. The musicians with him, Huw and Mark and Ellen – she knew them all- gave him solid backing, and when the harp went softly into its most poignant lament the whole audience was engrossed, the soft notes rising in skillful sorrow. The warm applause cheered Alex; some colour came back into his face and he caught her eyes through the dimness. 'This next one's for Katie,' he said.

People turned; someone whistled. Her father poked her in the ribs. 'Hey. He's too old for you.'

'Oh shut up!'

It was fast and vivid; a Welsh reel she knew well, though not the name of it, and when it was finished in a screech of the fiddle she was sure he was all right, that he would get through it now.

Listeners were crowding in through the flap; she saw Mick there with Rowan standing behind him and waved, though he didn't see her. But the woman smiled back, her green eyes sharp and laughing.

49

A few songs came next, with Huw's strong voice; then some longer pieces, and a Gaelic hymn. The only time Alex faltered was when he looked up at the doorway. Katie noticed it at once, halfway through the eerie old song 'She Moved through the Fair,' with the long skirl of the Irish pipes, clear and strange, and Huw singing the threat of the dead woman coming back for her lover. 'It will not be long, love,' he sang, 'till our wedding day.'

And the pipes jarred. Just for a note, but she heard it, and saw that Alex had been watching Rowan, a puzzled glance that had lasted a fraction too long. He didn't look up again.

When it was all over, the applause was loud. Katie looked over but the doorflap was empty, and she frowned. Where was Mick now? He always seemed to be vanishing these days.

She waited outside till Martin and the others had finished talking to Alex, slapping him on the back, teasing him; then she went in to the empty tent. He was standing by the harp, hands in pockets, looking down at it.

'Not bad,' she said, slyly.

He turned, flushed and relieved. 'Thanks to you.'

'I didn't do anything. It was you.'

He nodded, as if to convince himself. 'Yes. Me.'

Walking across the Field, the wind blowing his hair out, he said, 'Was that Mick, who came in near the end, with that girl?'

She nodded.

'You called her Rowan?'

'Yes.'

'Who is she?'

Katie looked up in surprise. 'I don't know.'

'But Mick knows her?'

'She says so.'

For some reason the questions made her feel irritated. They bought ice-creams, and unpeeling hers she said, 'I'd better get back.'

He hesitated, scratching the side of his face. Then he said, 'Katie. Will you show me where the crop circle is?'

'What, now?'

'Yes.' He shook his head. 'While I've got the courage.'

She wondered what he meant, but didn't ask. 'We'll have to be quick.'

She led the way. They didn't speak till they'd crossed the lawns of the Hall and reached the gate by the wood. Mr Carter came storming out of it, a girl with a camera trailing behind him. He looked hot and furious.

'Hi,' Katie said. 'Can we go in?'

Mick's father glared down at her. 'Something's going on here, and I'm damned if I'm going to be made a fool of like this. Put that message round the Field, Katie!' Shoving past them he stalked off through the tourists.

Alex watched him, looking worried. 'What does he mean?'

'I don't know. Come on.'

They walked along the corn-edge. In the heat the field shimmered, the golden husks whispering, barely bending.

When they stopped Alex stared. 'Where is it?' he asked, uneasy.

But Katie was still with surprise, her fingers quite cold, even in this heat.

The cornfield was perfect, a sea of gold, all the way to the hedgerow.

As silently as it had come, the circle had vanished.

SEVEN

He wandered high, he wandered low,
He wandered late and early,
Until he came to that on water,
And there he spied his ladie.

TRAD.

There was a wide gravel walk, and it ended with a round fountain. In the centre of the tree-reflections Apollo stood, lyre in hand, his other arm outstretched, as if reaching for something. On each side of him stone dolphins spouted shimmering arcs of water, that gushed over the basin and dripped into the circular pool.

Mick sat on the edge, swishing his hand in it.

He was hot and restless. At his feet the flute lay shining in its case but he couldn't touch it. Instead he watched the god's grave young face in the water. Opposite, Katie sat with her feet in the pool, the hem of her long dress soaked and floating. She was glaring at him. 'Have you heard a word I've said?'

'Yes,' he lied.

She raised an eyebrow. 'Well you don't seem much bothered. Think about it Mick! How can a circle of bent corn stand back up again, and so straight there's not a sign of damage? Because there wasn't. I got right in and looked. And those lights we saw! Something's going on — aren't you even curious about what it is?'

He forced a smile. 'All right! I'm curious.' But he wasn't. He was confused. He didn't want to think about the earth–lights, because when he did his mind always shifted back to Rowan on her white horse, saying that he had called her. He wanted to tell Katie about that, wanted it badly, but looking at her now, re-doing one of her tiny plaits in the sunshine, he couldn't. It didn't seem anything he could talk about in the daylight.

And then there was that Branch. If he listened hard he could hear it even now, the chime of it, going on and on somewhere deep in his head as if it had never stopped echoing there. A single, pure note, breathtakingly beautiful.

'*Michael!*'

He looked up, startled.

Katie was grinning, her plait finished; his father standing there looking at him oddly. 'Did you tell them?'

With a shock, he knew minutes had gone by. Even the shadows had shifted.

'Tell who?'

Mr Carter breathed out with strained patience. 'What's the matter with you? Your last group. About the special offers in the tea-room.'

'Oh. Yes.' He shrugged, confused. 'I think I did.'

'Well, none of them went in there.'

Suddenly Mick was sick of it; he picked the flute up, snapping the case shut irritably. 'Sorry. Taken a chunk out of your profits, I suppose.'

His father flushed. 'Those profits pay our bills. Don't forget that!'

'How can I? You never stop talking about them.'

He walked off quickly but his father said, 'You've

53

always had money, that's your trouble. When you're desperate for some . . .'

Mick swung furiously. 'What makes you think I will be!'

'Musicians always are! It's not a real life . . .'

'It's real enough for me!' Mick was hot with rage; Katie watched anxiously, her feet cold in the water.

'You've got no confidence in me at all!' he yelled. 'You've no idea what I can do . . . could do. All you do is put me down, all the time, whatever I do or say! I'm sick of it, just sick of it. You've never even listened to me play, have you? Not once!'

Then he was gone, ducking under the yew branches, burning.

Katie pulled her feet out and jumped up.

'What's got into him these days?' Mr Carter muttered. 'It's as if he can't bring himself to talk to me. Does he think the whole world revolves around him?'

Katie was pulling her shoes on. 'I'll go after him.'

He looked at her. 'I suppose you think he's right.'

'He really wants it . . .'

'Yes, Katie, but it might just be a phase. I can't let him waste his life.'

She shifted, uncomfortable, not wanting to make things worse.

'It's this Fair,' he burst out, irritably. 'I always loathe this wretched Fair. It unsettles everything! Every summer, no order to it, springing up overnight, all these oddballs, dropouts, a rag-tag of strangers, and it's worse than ever this year. I don't mean your people, of course.'

'No.' She hid a smile. 'Anyway, at least the crop circle's gone.'

54

'That's another thing . . .' But as he said it, a sudden sound rose around them; a deep humming as if hundreds of bees were swarming.

Katie turned. 'What's that?'

Michael Carter rubbed his hot hair. 'If it's that wretched sound system . . .'

'We're too far from the Field. Besides . . .' she turned, listening, 'it's so close, as if it's right here.'

The buzz disturbed them, fading and rising; a deep zizzing summer sound of hot fields and midges, vibrating the water-drops on the basin's edge. And then, between one second and another, it was gone, the bird song sounding oddly too loud.

Rowan met Mick at the entrance to her stall. 'I felt you coming,' she said, rubbing one earring.

Herbs were smoking in bowls over some candles, their pungent fumes hanging in the warm air. Still angry, Mick looked down, fidgeting with the flute.

'You haven't been playing,' she said, looking at him narrowly. 'That's not like you. Why not Mick? Don't you trust me?'

'I don't know,' he mumbled, picking up bits of crystal.

Behind them an accordion started up noisily; a group of Morris men began to dance with a crash of bells.

'Don't worry about your father,' she said.

'I'm not.' He looked round, nervous. 'I just . . . Can I buy another one of your chimes? The other one hasn't got the right note, somehow.'

Rowan nodded, her eyes green and mocking. 'I see,' she said, gravely. 'This time you'd better choose your own, then.'

He went further back, into the dimness, and reached

up and touched them, and they all chinked and hummed and tinkled, the notes drifting round him like the smoke, so that the bright field outside was misted and distant. All the greenness of leaves seemed to come out of them, the twistings of ancient wood, slow growths of lichen on branches. Deep, fecund sounds gathered round him, and the music he heard among them was a low flute, far-off and eerie, playing mysterious breathy notes, a wordless wood-music.

The noises of the Fair were faint; they sounded bizarre to him now, crass and over-sharp and out of key. This was the music he wanted, but even as he hungered after it it faded, and the clank of the Morris bells grated on his nerves.

Rowan was close to him, one hand lightly on his shoulder. 'Choose,' she whispered in his ear. He picked a wind-chime blindly off the rail and in the mirror he saw her smile, her moon-earrings glinting, and in all the mirrors and candlesticks of the stall other faces watched him, leering, tangled in branches and bines.

She took the chimes and wrapped them in purple tissue paper.

'It was a good choice, Mick,' she said. 'Don't be afraid of us, or what we can do.' She gave him the parcel. 'Enjoy it. We'll be waiting for you.'

The clamour of the accordion tormented him. He tipped a few coins into her hand.

Hurrying away, walking quickly not to see Katie, he noticed Alex.

The harper was watching him from the chairs under the trees; their eyes met briefly. Mick jerked his gaze away; instantly he ran, before the man could get up, pushing through the crowd, under the banners, into the car park, away.

All afternoon he walked, anywhere, nowhere, wandering the lawns and deep into the woods, through the Rose Walks and Herb Garden, round the lake, watching the ducks swoop and glide to the children who fed them bread. He sat in the Hothouse for an hour, the humidity soaking him, the great cacti silent in the airless hush, flies buzzing in the white-coated skylights. And as he sat there he looked down at the flute, shimmering in its velvet grooves.

Katie found Alex waiting for her by the forge.

'More repairs?' she grinned, but when he glanced at her he seemed distant, as if he'd been remembering far-off things.

'I wanted to talk to you.'

'Go ahead.' She sat in the grass, brushing off bees. He crouched next to her.

'Has Rowan been at this Fair before?'

She shrugged. 'Her again. I don't think so. There are lots of new people this year.'

He nodded, his long fingers shredding grass. 'I'd noticed. Strangers. Jugglers. Acrobats. Always about, always listening.'

Curious, Katie watched him. 'You do know her, don't you? Look, is she trouble in any way?'

He stood up, as if she'd alarmed him. 'I told you. The one I knew was different – she had long hair, she was older. At first she was older. It's not the same woman. It can't be.'

He turned but almost at once swung back, the sun slanting on the small metal disc he wore. 'Katie, what does Mick want most in the world?'

She laughed. 'To be a musician, of course.'

He was silent.

'There's something you're not telling me,' she said.

Their eyes met.

The harper looked tired. There was a longing in his eyes that frightened her.

'Warn him,' he whispered. 'Tell him it's not supposed to be that easy.'

Mick clanged the gate behind him.

In the late afternoon glow the wood-shadow was long; already the cornfield was edged with mist. The great golden expanse spread itself before him; reckless, he plunged in.

This time he walked straight, not caring, rustling through the chest-high crop, stumbling on furrows, snapping the stiff stems until all around him the corn whispered and rippled and stirred, and he felt cut off from the world, from the Fair with its garish noise and colours.

Over his head, house martins swooped and screeched.

He took the flute out of its case; it was hot, and his hands were too, making steamy streaks as he fitted the mouthpiece on, twisting it, lifting it to his lips, the warm touch disturbing him.

Then, at last, he let himself play, a long trill of relief, and all the notes came whistling out, a fast, fierce rage of music, so ready and confident that his heart raced with the power and fear of it. It was him playing, he knew that; not the old useless Mick, stubbing his fingers with nerves – this was the real him, the buried ability he'd always had and never let himself use, a fierce cruel talent that burned him. Somewhere there were other players too, all round him; pipes and fiddles and dulcimer and drums, all in harmony, all rising to a ferocity that made the baked earth tremble. The corn stirred; it churned and shimmered and danced with him. As he watched, it swirled into the sorcerous shapes of the music, a great pattern of song rippling out from his feet in rings and arcs and spirals, far out to the hedgerows; an electric energy that made the hairs along his arms tingle. He was doing this, he was making it happen, he knew, so that he closed his eyes and played on with them all, into the darkness, into the night, and it was hours later when he stood there and realised the music had ended, the energy had gone.

He was standing under a sky full of stars, facing the moon, a narrow yellow moon rising over him.

Weariness soaked him. He felt drained, his whole strength spent. It cost him an effort even to turn his head.

All around him, far into the dark, the corn lay flat in wild patterns; spirals, great geometric shapes. Above its silence moths fluttered and a few bats careered crazily in the purple sky, zig-zagging after invisible beetles.

Beyond, in hedges, high in trees, squatting on logs, lying in the corn, all the strangers of the Fair grinned back at him, troupes of tiny grotesque men, beautiful girls, tall, strangely-dressed harpers and jugglers and drummers, and beyond them uglier shapes, misshapen, lost in shadows.

Among them stood Rowan, tall as a queen, her dress dark blue, scattered with stars. When he saw her he laughed, and she laughed with him, rich and free.

'Welcome to the Host of the Air, Mick,' she said.

59

PART TWO

The Host of the Air

EIGHT

O where ha' you been, Lord Randal, my son?
And where ha' you been, my handsome young man?

TRAD.

In the dim tent only the candles flickered, an arch of them, their tiny warm flames lighting the side of the storyteller's face.

'Long ago,' he said, 'a man was chosen. He had to be young and he had to be fair. Early in the year when the ground was cold and hard after the winter, his was the task of planting the first seeds. He was dedicated to the land. He was crowned the Corn King.'

Someone stirred in the crowd. Katie eased her knees up, the tartan shawl warm around her shoulders. The sweet sticky smell of doughnuts wafted from outside the tent.

The storyteller was a young man, with a keen, intense face. He looked out at his shadowed listeners. 'All spring, as the green shoots grew, the Corn King lived in luxury. Everything he wanted he could have. The finest clothes, linen, silks and satins. The finest food and wines. The best harpers to play for him. A great house all of his own. And as the man lived well, so the corn grew, tall and yellow and strong. They were one. Their destinies were linked.'

He paused. A faint breeze moved the canvas. Out on the dark Field fires crackled; someone giggled, a low mockery that distracted Katie. She scratched her bare toes.

The storyteller's eyes were bright in a mask of flamelight and shadow. His voice was lower now, more ominous.

'Finally, the corn was ready. All the tribes gathered for the harvest, the precious grain that would keep them alive through the bitter winter. The Corn King was brought out.

The one that waited for him was old; she was Death and Winter, all the harshness of the cold unfeeling Earth. She carried a sickle of whetted stone. Youth and Age, Summer and Winter, faced each other.

And the Corn King was cut down there, among the crop, so that his red blood flowed back into the land, deep into the furrows, enriching it. The corn too, was cut. The harvest was over. Next year, a new King would be chosen, and from the death of one, new life would spring up. But the last sheaf was kept, for in it the spirit of the corn lived. It was knotted and plaited into a figure, strange and faceless. And it was kept safe, until next year.'

From his finger he swung the corn dolly. There was a whole stall of them out on the Field, Katie knew.

For a moment there was silence. Then the crowd applauded, quietly. People stretched; places were changed. A few beercans sparked open.

Stiff, Katie got up and hobbled to the back. There were more performers left but she was tired and yawning; muttering goodnight to a few people she got to the door-flap and pushed through it, into the warm night. Someone caught up with her.

'Hi there.'

Turning, she saw Sandy.

'Hello!' Almost automatically, she looked round for the baby.

The tall girl giggled. 'Anna's not here. Michael's babysitting. Do him good to change a few nappies.'

Katie grinned. Sandy looked young, with her long straight hair swinging.

'We don't see you on the Field that often.'

'Oh, I usually walk Anna round in the pushchair most afternoons to watch the dancers, but it's a change to get a night off.' She looked longingly over at the sizzling doughnut stand. 'Can I buy you one?'

Katie thought about her supper, waiting in the caravan.

'Go on, then,' she said.

They strolled over, to the back of a small queue. The Lammas Field was dark, only some of the stalls still lit up with strings of lightbulbs or oil-lamps that glowed behind the canvas.

'That last one was a weird story,' Sandy said.

Katie nodded. 'It's traditional.'

'What a surprise!'

'No, I mean for the Fair. They tell it every year. Because of the Ritual.'

They shuffled on for a few steps. Then Sandy said casually, 'Where's Mick?'

Katie shrugged. 'Who knows?' She'd meant to say it calmly, but even she could hear the resentment. Sandy looked interested.

'Oh, it's just he's avoiding me. I haven't really talked to him for days – not since the crop circles started again. He always seems to be with Rowan and her friends – an odd bunch most of them. Or playing. He's playing in everything – every ceilidh, all the sessions, never seems to stop. I mean that's good, but,' she shrugged, rolling her shawl up, 'it's a bit obsessive.'

Sandy paid for the doughnuts. They were hot and soft, wonderfully chewy. After a mouthful, she brushed lumps of sugar from her lips.

'I wondered what he was up to. I'll tell him to slow down. I was thinking at breakfast about how peaky he looked; he's been missing meals. Too much junk food.' She giggled, taking another bite.

Katie nodded. Not far away Alex had come out of the beer tent carrying a fiddle, and turned quickly away from them into the rows of stalls.

'Who's he?' Sandy asked, noticing.

'Someone else who's avoiding me.' She licked her fingers. 'Thanks for that. But I'd better get home.'

'Will you be all right?' Sandy looked round at the darkening Fair. 'I'm surprised how Jean lets you walk round at night.'

Katie pushed her hair back. 'This is the Fair. We know each other.'

But as she waved at the Field's edge and turned between the dim banners she wondered if that was true any more. Alex was right. Something was happening to the Fair. There were too many strangers — too many people here at night, camp-fires that came and went, musicians no one knew. For days they'd been arriving, till suddenly the Field seemed full of strange faces. Very strange, some of them.

Crossing the dim carpark she opened the gate and walked down the track. A long yellow tape had been strung out on sticks; now it flapped loose in long loops, but she knew the way even in the dark. The caravan lights gleamed through the trees ahead.

The path went down into a hollow. There were usually blue lightbulbs strung here but they didn't seem to be lit tonight.

The hollow was dark, a little steep.

Katie took two steps. Then she stopped.

Between her and the caravan field, the copse was a silent gather of trees.

She took a slow breath; sweat prickling on her neck.

The trees were waiting for her.

She knew it was stupid. She could see the van lights, but the wood seemed a sudden dark threat; even as she made herself walk on, she knew it. Something rustled. Above her a whistle sounded, low and cunning.

Swallowing hard, Katie marched on. The trees were thick; there were too many, more than there ought to be. When she came to the lights she stared down at them in disbelief.

Not the caravans.

A circle of lightbulbs lay on the floor of the wood like a mockery of the corn circles; torn down, the bulbs that should have been lighting the path. They lay there, green and red and blue, their garish light thrown on tree-roots and bracken, and on a scatter of small white pieces that she crouched down to, and saw with a quiver of coldness, were bones. Frail, picked clean.

Something laughed at her shoulder.

She turned. Faces of fear stared at her, with bent noses, squinting eyes, hair like black straw. There were ranks and rows of them, swinging and laughing, eyes bright.

Chilled, hands clenched, Katie stood frozen.

It took her a long time, but at last she reached out; made herself reach out and touch one, spinning it on its string. Her back was icy with sweat.

The masks all looked back at her. Behind their eye-slits, nothing but darkness.

Suddenly she ran, fast along the path, and it kinked and twisted and almost seemed to fling her out against the first van. The Frobisher's, with its painted wheels.

Breathless, she stopped there, and stared back into the restless, creaking wood.

Fear had entered the Fair. It had come slowly, creeping up on them all, but now it was here. She could feel it hammering in her heart, in all the trees, hung with their mocking, spinning faces.

It was only later that night, curled in restless sleep, that the astonishing memory surfaced and jerked her wide awake staring up at the dim ceiling.

The cable of lightbulbs had been torn down, broken off.

And yet all the bulbs had been shining.

'You can do this,' Rowan urged.

Mick looked up at the windows of the flat, high in the East wing. 'I'll try,' he said doubtfully.

She tapped his arm. 'Now. Tell him. We want you with us.'

He turned away from her and went in. All the way along the corridors and up the Great Stair he felt her still with him, among the dim bowls of lavender pot-pourri: a shadow somewhere up ahead, glimpsed in windows and picture-glass and mirrors, and as he passed the Damask Room he saw her there in the moonlight, swirling the long silken folds of the bedcurtains in delight.

At the flat, he let himself in quietly.

His father was watching TV, his feet up on the coffee table. Maybe he'd been asleep; now he glanced over dully at Mick, who poured a drink quietly from the fridge.

'You missed supper.'

'I had something on the Field.' It was a lie, but Mick didn't care. Suddenly he was too tired even to think, and thirsty, as if he hadn't drunk for days. He dumped the glass on the table and turned.

'I won't be doing the tours for a bit.'

His father stared. 'What!'

'I've got a lot to do. They're teaching me all of it, accordion, whistles, pipes. There's so much to learn.'

His father struggled up, furious, but before he could say anything Mick was gone, slamming the door, hearing the sharp note of it ring in his head like a pain. Stumbling down the corridor he knew everything had its music now. Why hadn't he noticed them before, the sharp squeaks of the boards, the tiny descending chords of the water splashed on his face?

He stood in his bedroom, hauled the window open and looked down, hands on the sill.

From the smooth lawns Rowan looked up at him, her dress stolen pale silk from the Damask Room, her hair glinting with silver.

'All done?' she whispered.

'All done.'

Some of the others gathered round her, silent, coming out of nowhere. He knew them all now, heard the squeal and warm-up of the pipes with a smile.

Wearily, he turned and climbed into bed.

All night the seven wind-chimes over his head jangled through his dreams.

NINE

My breast it is as cold as clay
My breath smells earthly strong;
And if you kiss my cold clay lips
Your days they won't be long.

TRAD.

The bus was full. If it hadn't been, Katie thought, he wouldn't have come and sat by her. She smiled to herself, switching off the Walkman. Now he was trapped for twenty minutes at least. Time enough to get plenty of answers.

Alex seemed to be thinking that himself. He sat down and dumped a rucksack between his feet.

'Been shopping?' he asked quietly.

She tapped the plastic carrier. 'Birthday money. I thought I'd spend it in the big town.' They both grinned. Marlbury was hardly a street long.

The bus shuddered into life, slewing away from the stop.

'What about you?' she asked.

He looked up the aisle, not at her. 'Hospital. I'm still an out-patient.'

She nodded, trying not to look too interested. 'The Infirmary?'

He hesitated. Then he said 'St Martin's.'

That silenced her. St Martin's was a psychiatric

70

unit. She glanced at him sidelong, wondering if she should have known since that panic attack outside the tent. Some sort of breakdown, then. A few comments Martin Frobisher had made flitted through her memory.

Outside the window the fields flashed by, heavy with their crops. The harvest had started already on some farms, and stood in great roundels and swirls; enormous wheels of vegetation strange under the blue sky. Beyond, the chalk downs rose, ominous with beeches and barrows.

Alex glanced at the Walkman. 'Don't let me keep you from the music.'

'You're not.' He shook his head, smiling.

The bus was hot; a fly banged against the glass. At the next stop three hikers got on with enormous rucksacks; they piled them in the baggage rack and stood, swaying, as the bus rumbled up the narrow lanes.

Katie pondered her reflection. She wanted to know about Alex, but this wasn't a good place. She watched his reflection in the window. He stared ahead, a little embarrassed, and she saw how his hand felt for the small disc on the chain, turning it in his fingers as if that was a habit that calmed him.

'It must be a strain for you,' she ventured.

'What?'

'The Fair. Coming back.'

'The music's my livelihood,' he muttered. Then he said 'Katie, please . . .'

'Something's wrong at the Fair.' She turned to him, urgent, glad to have someone to tell. 'And with Mick. He's turning into a stranger, drifting away from us. I think you know who Rowan is, and I think you ought to tell me. You owe me a favour.'

He was sweating, maybe with the heat. Irritably he wiped his cheek with the back of one hand. Two women in front gossiped loudly; leaves rattled along outside the window like a warning.

Then he said, 'Look. What happened to me. I don't know any more whether I dreamed most of it, hallucinated, whatever. I've never been able to tell them, not properly. These doctors, these analysts with their degrees and therapies and tests, what do they know about the music, how it eats at you, what you'd do for it?'

She said nothing.

'The people at the Fair, they know. You know, in a way.'

'I'm no musician.'

'But your friend is.' He twisted the disc, looking so agitated she wanted to tell him it didn't matter. But before she could he was speaking again, his voice low.

'It started years ago. I wanted to play, but we didn't have much money for lessons. So I learned from friends, went to a folk club, got into a band, the usual thing. I was ambitious; I knew I could be good, but I never really believed in myself, not as a composer, or as one of those that people would say was brilliant, that they'd go miles to hear. I wanted it, more than anything, but I never thought I'd do it. Until I met her.'

Katie watched. His eyes were distant, remembering.

'She had long, black hair, a tangle of it. I was working in a garden centre then, and I hated it. One day it just all seemed too much. I was fed up and desperate, almost sick with despair. I looked up, and she was standing there, by a fountain. She'd have had to walk past me to get there, but she hadn't. She just appeared. I think I knew from the start that she wasn't mortal, wasn't real like the rest of us.'

Uneasy, Katie laughed. 'Not mortal?'

'No.' He was ominously calm.

The sun was burning her bare arm through the window, but she hardly felt it. The bus swung out on to the main road again.

Alex said, 'I know what you're thinking, but I'm not crazy. They have many names. They call themselves the Host of the Air, the Sidhe, the Midnight Court. She leads them. She can do great things, Katie. They taught me to play like a sorcerer; I could do anything. Sometimes I was afraid to pick up the harp, such music would come out of it. I left everything; my job, family, friends. I didn't eat, I didn't sleep. Nothing mattered to me but the music. Her music. She owned me.'

The sun's glare was scorching. Katie put her hand up to shield her face. 'But that wasn't Rowan,' she whispered. 'Was it?'

He glanced at her, then past her, and his eyes suddenly widened. 'We've missed the stop!'

Jumping up, he rang the bell.

The abrupt change of mood jolted her; for a second she felt bewildered, had to drag herself to the present and scramble for the plastic bag that had slid well under the seat in front.

When she got down to the door of the bus the driver was shrugging at Alex. 'Sorry son. There's an articulated on my tail and nowhere to pull in. You'll have to wait till the crossroads.'

When the bus pulled away they were standing on a tiny pocket of grass by a phone box. Behind them a lane ran back between uncut hedges; to left and right the main road stretched away, cars searing along it.

'We'll have to walk. Give me your bag.'

She handed it over; he crammed it into the rucksack and swung it over his shoulders. 'Sorry,' he muttered. 'This is my fault.'

'I didn't notice either.'

She was desperate to find out more, but the traffic was too loud; they could barely hear each other. They started to walk back along the main road, Alex first, facing the cars. There was no pavement, just a hedge with nettles that stung them. Horns blared; Katie's hair flew wild in the slipstream.

'It's too dangerous,' she yelled.

She saw him shrug. 'What else can we do?'

They were well over a mile from the main lodge gates of Stokesey, where the bus stop was. Lorries tore past them, making the tarmac tremble; the noise and dust and stink of exhaust fumes were unbearable. The speed and closeness of the cars numbed Katie at first, but as they went on a series of lorries almost drove her into the ditch. Alex turned, anxious. 'OK?'

'We'll be killed walking like this!'

She looked up. The hedge was a wall now, stone, tall but not smooth.

'That's the estate wall!' she yelled. 'Let's get over it!'

He backed against it as a red car flashed by. 'All right. Go on.'

She grabbed the stones, stuck her foot in a crack and hauled herself up, grinning. This was better, this was wild.

A car tooted; she ignored it. Climbing up she swung her legs over, ducking under the low branches of larch that hung over the wall. Then carefully, slithering and slipping and finally jumping through a mass of cracking twigs, she made her way down.

It was instantly quieter. She could breathe; a deep calm of pine-sap and moss.

The rucksack landed with a thump; looking up she saw Alex letting himself down from branch to branch, awkward, scraping down the wall. He fell and picked himself up. They grinned at each other, then Katie giggled.

'Well it's better than getting run over.'

'A lot.'

'Hands OK?'

He rubbed them together. 'Harper's hands are tough.'

Katie dragged a twig from her hair, looking round. 'Right. So where are we?'

They were in a gloomy plantation of dank conifers and larches that grew right up against the wall. Underfoot, the ground was soft and springy with needles, a deep brown mattress of them. It was easy to walk between the trunks, with no undergrowth. Katie set off, keeping more or less parallel with the road; swinging the rucksack up, Alex followed.

For a while they went silent, until the roar of the road had softened and faded. Then she said 'Are you going to tell me the rest?'

He glanced at her. 'Don't give up, do you?'

Tangling a plait round one finger she said 'If you don't want to . . .'

'Of course I don't want to.' For a moment he sounded angry. When he went on, she knew he was forcing himself to get it over.

'There's not much to say. I was living a dream. Most of

75

it I don't even remember. Concerts, festivals, the music always going on in my head. Like the Branch.'

'The what?'

If he heard her he made no sign, bending low under the leaves. 'And then I woke up. In one clear moment.'

He stepped over a fallen log that was rotting to pieces, pacing on so fast Katie could hardly keep up.

'It was after a gig one night. She was outside with the others; for once they'd left me alone. I could hear her laughing. I thought the audience had all gone, but when I looked up there was still someone there, shadowy, three rows back. He was elderly, some sort of clergyman, looking at me hard. Finally, he came up to the stage. I was clearing up, trying to ignore him, but as soon as he spoke I felt a sort of calm shoot through me, as if something had gone, some terrible tense bubble had burst. He just said 'Son, what are you doing to yourself?'

That was all. But he sounded so kind, Katie. And all of a sudden I realised that no one had spoken to me like that for years.'

He stopped, abruptly, one hand against a treetrunk. 'I looked up and saw my face reflected in the glass at the back of the staging and I hardly recognised myself. I was so thin, so worn away. Then I knew that I was fading, that she was drawing the energy out of me, feeding off me. I could see her through the gap in the door, her hair black and glossy, her lips red and full. She was younger. I was sure she was younger.'

Katie shook her head. She didn't know what to believe. Gently she said, 'What did you do?'

Alex walked on, slower. The conifers were darker here; flies rose in clouds. 'The priest gave me this. He just pressed it into my hand. "I'll pray for you," he said, and he went.'

The harper's fingers turned the disc at his neck. 'It's iron. They hate iron. As soon as she came back she sensed it, and all the spell came off her. I saw her properly, saw she was beautiful and cold, that there was nothing human in her at all.'

He brushed under the low branches. 'I can't tell you all of it. It was hell, but I got free. It almost cost me my sanity because all I wanted was the music, and I still do. You're never really safe . . .'

Katie touched his arm, and he almost jumped, as if he had forgotten her. She stopped and faced him.

'Is this the woman Mick has met?'

'No.' He shook his head firmly. 'She's different.'

'But if what you say is true she could look like anyone.'

'It can't be. I'd know.' He pushed past her, walking on.

'Maybe you do know,' she said.

He looked back, silent.

After half an hour they passed the tiny lane that led up to Tom's cottage. Now Katie knew where they must be, though she'd never been in this corner of the estate. It was quiet here among the trees, except for the faintest drift of music somewhere ahead, that she thought must be from the Field. Alex seemed hardly to hear it, lost in old memories.

Then they stepped out into a dark clearing that stank of something dead. Katie jammed her hand over her mouth in disgust. 'Oh God, look at that.'

The fox-skin had been nailed wide to a great oak; other gruesome things hung above it, that might once have been birds, magpies or crows, rotten now, lumps of gristle and feather swarming with hundreds of black flies that rose in a hissing cloud.

Instantly, as if he knew they had stepped into some trap, Alex looked back. The path was gone. All the trees seemed to have stepped together.

It was gloomy here. Soft white growths sprouted from the spongy floor, as if rotting things decayed underneath.

Katie stared round. 'I wouldn't have thought Tom would do this.'

'Not Tom.' The harper was tense, as if some old nightmare was creeping back over him.

She stepped out, and beyond him, saw the opening.

It was a black mouth between upright stones; at first she thought it was a cave, or the entrance into some Underworld. It was huge; it reminded her of the mouth of Hell, steaming, in an old painting. Then, in the gloom, her eyes made out the shape of it, a long barrow, running back into the wood, the trees springing out of its neglected humps. Its stones leaned, like great teeth, green with moss, the ancient spirals on them weathered almost to nothing.

'It's a long barrow.'

'It's a hollow hill.' Alex looked round, cold with fear. 'Katie, we have to get away from here . . .'

'It's a bit grim, I admit. Mick never told me this was here.'

He was silent; she looked round and said, 'Alex?'

When he answered, he didn't speak to her. He spoke to the tall stone on the left, its upright shape masked with ivy, and Katie felt a chill of dread at the desperation in his voice.

'Don't do this to me,' he said. 'Don't let me hear it again.'

TEN

'O where have you been my long, long love
This seven long years and mair?'
'O I'm come to seek my former vows
Ye granted me before.'

                                    TRAD.

The woman moved, coming out of the shadows. Alex saw she held the Branch, and its tiny silver bells made a shiver of notes. Despite the talisman round his neck, he felt their power stab through his every nerve. He clenched his hands. Cold sweat prickled down his back.

He had forgotten how beautiful she was. For a moment she was there as he had known her, dark and earthy, a gold necklace gleaming, and then her outline rippled into Rowan, taller, her hair short and red, her face mocking.

'You don't have to hear it again,' she said. 'You've never stopped hearing it. I don't forgive those who try to escape me, Alex.'

He glanced at Katie. The girl stood warily in the dark clearing. She was watching him, a little scared. 'Who are you talking to?' she murmured.

He looked back. 'Rowan. She's standing in front of us. Can't you see her?'

Even before she answered, he knew it was hopeless. He'd been through this many times before.

79

'There's nothing there.' Katie laughed, as if she felt foolish. 'Come on. I don't like this place.'

He didn't move.

Rowan came, and reached out to brush the hair from his forehead; then she shivered oddly and drew back, glaring coldly at the iron disc.

'If you didn't have that thing I'd let you come back with me. Maybe I'll do it anyway. You still want to come, don't you?'

'What about the boy?' he whispered.

She smiled, happily, sitting on a low stone, leaning back, her dress trailing in the nettles. 'Ah, Mick. What a find he is! So young, so eager to learn. He's as hungry as you were. And the music runs almost as deep in him as it did in you.'

'Does,' he muttered.

She tipped her head. 'I know. It's not too late Alex. You can come back.'

'No.' The word was almost a whisper. He knew Katie was staring at him.

'You'll never be anything without me. You'll only ever be second-rate. Mediocre. And you know that's true.'

He pulled back, shaking. Frightened, Katie caught his arm. 'You look awful. Do you feel ill?'

Behind her, through her, like a ghost in a nightmare, Rowan watched him.

'And I might even let the boy go,' she whispered.

Instantly, Alex broke out of Katie's grip and turned, walking fast, stumbling into the trees, pushing through branches, never looking back.

'Hang on!' She caught up with him. 'What's the matter! Tell me!'

But he wouldn't, not until they came abruptly out from the wood and there was the great blue lake spread out before them, a shimmering crescent, the high clouds drifting over its surface, the green lawns and elegant facade of Stokesey beyond, all gables and windows.

Breathless, Alex stopped and swung round. Katie came running up and stared at him angrily. 'What's the matter with you! I'm only trying to help.'

Fumbling in the rucksack, he pulled out her bag of shopping and pushed it into her arms. 'I'm sorry. I can't stay here.'

'Then we'll go to the Field . . .'

'I mean I'm leaving the Fair.'

Worried, Katie bit a nail. 'Look, I think you should talk to some of the others . . .'

He turned, then swung back. 'She'll entice me back. She's too strong for me.'

Katie shook her head in frustration. 'You said it was someone else!'

Fighting for calm he said, 'It was her. She just spoke to me.'

Cold now, Katie stepped back. Suddenly she felt afraid, felt that he was wild and strange and that she didn't know him at all.

'There was no one there,' she said firmly.

Alex was still. Then he swung the rucksack over his shoulder and walked down to the edge of the lake. For an awful moment she thought he would walk straight in, but instead he stood there, breathing deep, gazing out at the Hall, its gables and lawns. When he spoke he didn't look at her. 'Your friend is in great danger. You must warn him.'

'You could help me,' she said at random.

He gave her an unhappy smile. 'I'm sorry, Katie. He wouldn't want to hear it, though he might believe me. You don't, do you?'

She was hot and scared. 'I think . . .' Choosing her words carefully, she tried again. 'I think you might not have recovered as much as you thought.'

He nodded, gravely. 'I agree with you.'

'But you needn't leave the Fair. The music . . .'

He turned angrily. 'Goodbye, Katie. Thanks for your help.'

Bewildered, a little relieved, she let him walk away. Then, still clutching her plastic carrier, she turned and looked back into the dim, fly-blown clearing.

The black mouth of the burial chamber gaped open in the earth. Beside it, one green stone leaned.

The reporter fiddled with the tape machine, and clicked it off. 'Thanks. I think that'll be all now.'

'I'm glad to hear it.' Mr Carter mopped his neck with a tissue. 'Between you and me I'm sick of this. These things are frauds and if I find out who's responsible they'll be out of this Fair so fast . . .'

'You made that quite clear.' The woman looked out at the spirals and arcs of swirled corn. 'Still, you have to admit they're getting more and more spectacular. Isn't this the fourth since the Fair began?'

'And the last. Now, if you don't mind, I've got the estate to run.'

Leaving her with the cameraman, he turned and stalked through the gate. Bees fumbled in the thick clover of the hedge-bottom. On the lawns and gravel walks people were everywhere, picnicking; carrying bags, rugs, flasks, macs; pushing pushchairs. He picked up a sticky lolly-wrapper and dumped it in a bin, irritated, then waved one of the groundsmen out of the Rose Garden.

'When you've finished there, get a litter-picker and go round. This place looks like a tip.'

The man nodded, flapping dust from his thick gloves. 'Right, boss.'

'Have you seen my son?'

'Not since early.'

With a grunt he nodded, going back up through the hot terraces and the parterre, round to the side door, opening it with a key from the bunch.

Inside, the house was deliciously cool. A few rooms away, the low voice of a guide talked; Mr Carter peered in and saw the group clustered round the painting of Lady Elouisa Montague, possibly by Gainsborough, and one or two other visitors at the back, taking photos over the red tasselled ropes.

He backed out and closed the door.

What had got into the boy? At the busiest part of the season! But he knew what. It was the Fair. It was always the Fair.

Climbing the servants' stairs, with the frayed carpet that needed replacing, he ran through the events programme for that afternoon in his head. A week gone; the Fair half over. But the second week was the worst – packed with concerts and sessions and gigs, half of them unplanned, and then the Lammas Night at the end of it. But the Ritual was always the same. A barbaric fragment of some ancient horror. Followed by the concert, from which the group from Skye had cried off, so now that meant an afternoon of phoning round for replacements.

Someone was in his office. He opened the door and said 'Michael?' but it wasn't. It was Sandy, putting orange roses in a vase at the open window.

'Surprise,' she said.

'They smell nice.'

'From the roof.'

He sat down, dispirited, behind the sea of papers. 'Look at this. Where in God's name do I start?'

She came behind him and put her arms round his neck, kissing the top of his head absently. 'You should get a secretary.'

'The job's yours.'

'And.' She came round and looked at him. 'You should make it up with Mick.'

He frowned. 'Michael. I never see him. He's always off with Katie.'

'She says not. Says he's avoiding her.'

'In that case he's avoiding all of us. It gets worse every year.'

'Worse?'

He sorted papers, automatically. 'The Fair. Disturbs him, gets him restless. All the music.'

She sat on the edge of the desk. 'You know I don't like to interfere, Mike, but if his heart is so set on it . . .'

He looked up at her and sighed. 'Did I ever tell you,' he said suddenly, 'about when I was at school?'

'No!' She giggled. 'Did they have schools then?'

He grinned. 'Watch it. Do you know what I wanted to be? An archaeologist.'

'You!'

'Yes.' He smiled out of the window. 'With a beard and

84

muddy wellies and no money, living in a tent and knee-deep in Neolithic henges. Can you see me doing that?'

Sandy looked at him thoughtfully. 'So what changed your mind?'

'Oh, I don't know. Times were hard. My father lost his job. I changed courses; I needed something with money. Sometimes I kidded myself I'd go back and re-train, but after a while I knew I never would. And then I got married, and Michael came along . . . Things happen to you so fast. You end up as someone quite different.' He flapped the papers. 'I always swore I'd never end up behind a desk.'

She played with a pair of scissors. 'And yet you want Mick to?'

'I want him to be a success. And I know musicians – I see enough of them at this Fair. Tetchy, dirty, nervy, down at heel, no morals, no money, no future.' He looked up at her. 'I just want him to have a good life, Sandy. Is that so bad?'

'No.' She smiled and cut her fingernail. 'No. As long as he thinks the same.'

Mr Carter frowned. 'What does he know? He's just a kid.'

ELEVEN

Shee said 'Rise up, thou Child Waters,
I think thou art a cursed man.

TRAD.

'Mick? At the dance stage.' Calum McBride spun the vice open and took the thin beaten metal out.

'Playing or watching?' She already knew the answer.

'Playing.' Her father rubbed his newly-pierced ear. 'I'll tell you what, Katie, he's getting very good too. I'm surprised how good.'

She nodded, already walking away. 'Then I'd better go and listen.'

Warn him, Alex had said. She frowned out at the Fair.

It was four o'clock and still sultry. The Lammas Field was a mass of fading awnings, limp flags, the banners hanging in an airless heat. The crowds of the afternoon had thinned, but as she passed the commentary box with its bundles of flexes and wires, the loudspeakers told the Field in an echoing female voice that John Moore's grandmother was waiting for him by the hog roast.

Katie grinned.

Music was everywhere. An elderly man was singing Polish songs; a group from Morocco sat cross-legged on the grass making eerie tunes with instruments she hadn't even seen before, and behind the sizzle of evening fires and barking dogs there were drums beating, low and threatening and endlessly rhythmic.

The dance stage was empty, apart from some Appalachian dancers in jeans and clogs. Katie asked 'Where did the musicians go?'

'From the last set?' A boy pointed to a small tent pitched near the craft marquee. 'In there, some of them.'

She crossed the field towards it. It was new, a round black pavilion, looking strangely oriental and out of place, and though at first it was near, she was surprised at how she seemed to get no nearer to it, and when she'd threaded her way through the plastic tables and chairs outside the beer tent and looked up again, it even seemed to have shifted back among the marquees.

Clapping broke out behind her; a jerky fiddle and accordion erupted into a cheerful reel.

'Balloon?' a voice said slyly at her elbow.

Katie almost jumped.

A thin man in a jester's hat and orange T-shirt was hanging on to an enormous cloud of helium-filled balloons; they drifted and gusted above him, their shadows darkening the trampled grass.

'No, thanks.'

'Sure? Not ordinary balloons, these.' He had a long nose; his face was bony, thin lips wide in a leering smirk. She remembered she'd seen him talking to Rowan.

'I said, no.'

He jerked the strings down; suddenly the things bobbed and clustered round her, a threatening cloud, and she saw they weren't the usual hearts and cushions and Disney characters. Instead these had goblin faces, huge-lipped, one-eyed; hags with great noses and ears, hideous as the masks in the wood. There were animals too, snarling wolves, foxes, great black-beaked birds, and deep in the bobbing mass repulsive worm-like forms, women with cat's eyes, small goat-faces.

Annoyed and scared, Katie shoved them away, fighting her way out. 'You won't sell many of those,' she snapped.

He smirked at her. 'You'd be surprised, human child.'

Then she was away from him, walking fast in the sun that all at once didn't warm her. The black tent shimmered; she kept her eyes on it, ignoring the acrobatic troupe of small foreign-looking men tumbling over the grass towards her. When she reached the flap, she ducked hastily inside.

Then she stood still in astonishment.

The tent was far bigger than it had looked from outside. The music was deafening in here, a band of fiddle and bodhran and pipes, and Mick on flute, standing up, foot stamping.

Around her crowds of people were dancing; they danced wildly to the screaming rhythm of the jig, and as she pushed her way in, the bruised smell of the trampled grass was rich and fresh, the sunlight dimmed to a pale glow through the white canvas of the roof.

White?

She glanced up at it, puzzled.

Mick had seen her. His eyes followed her through the crowd, and just as she stumbled against the low stage the reel came to a sudden screeching end and the dancers whooped and stamped and clapped.

'What do you want?' he called down, grinning.

'You. To talk to you.'

He was different. She wasn't sure what it was, except that his face was thinner and there was a strange

88

emptiness in his eyes. He jumped down. 'What do you think?'

'The music? Great. But can't we get out of here? Who are all these people anyway?'

'Friends.' He waved the flute, a silver wand. 'All of these, and plenty more outside.'

The music broke out again; feverishly, he looked round. 'I'll have to get back.'

'But Mick . . . !'

He shrugged, laughing at her, backing through the crowd. Hands hoisted him eagerly up to the stage. Somebody grabbed Katie and whirled her into the dance. Breathless and furious she pulled away, but the rings of dancers held her, her hands were clutched tight and her hair tugged. The frenzy of the music seemed so loud it burst right into her skull and the rhythm pounded like her heart; or it was her heart, she thought, pulsing through her, and when it stopped in another endless storm of applause her mind seemed to click back from somewhere impossibly distant.

She was soaked with sweat; shaking with fatigue.

'Katie?' Mick grabbed her arm and dragged her to a table. 'Have a drink.'

Rubbing her hot face she looked at the food; delicate cakes, fruit, drinks in long iced glasses. It looked inviting, but she turned away and said 'Let's get outside.'

'But . . .'

'Outside, Mick! Now!'

Catching his sleeve she pulled him through the throng, shoving people aside rudely and with growing anger. A man turned and smiled at her, showing sharp white teeth.

At the door Mick made her stop. 'Wait, Katie! Please . . .'

'What's the matter with you?' she seethed. 'I just want to talk to you!'

Turning back she thumped straight into Rowan.

The tall woman stood inside the doorway, as if she had just come through it. On each side of her a dark, grim-looking man stood, identical as twins, their long manes of hair rough as a wolf's.

'Hello, Katie,' she said calmly.

'I'm taking Mick out for some air.' With an effort Katie made her voice sound polite. 'He looks pale, don't you think?'

To her astonishment, Rowan reached out and smoothed the hair back from his forehead, looking at him critically. 'Perhaps he does, a little. Go with her Mick. We'll see you later.'

She winked at him, secretly, then walked into the crowd.

Outside Mick blinked, as if even the late sunshine blinded him. Suddenly he seemed tired, all his energy used up. 'What's the time?' he muttered.

'Fivish.' Katie looked at her watch, then shook it in amazement. 'Half past six! How long were we in there?'

'Time goes fast when the music starts,' he said quietly.

She looked at him curiously. 'Well she likes you, doesn't she. You'd think she was your mother, the way she acts.'

He gave her a cold glance, and stalked away. Katie followed, annoyed with herself. That had been a stupid thing to say.

By the beer tent he seemed to have calmed down.

She bought drinks and he gulped his as if he hadn't drunk anything for hours, and then had another. Sitting on the hay bales she said, 'Sorry.'

He nursed the cold can in his hands for a while. Then he said, 'It doesn't matter. I never knew my mother anyway.' He looked out at the tents and stalls. 'I don't seem to have seen you for ages.'

'Well, I've been here. Where have you been?'

He looked at her strangely. 'Playing. I think.'

'And working?'

'No. I've given that up.'

Amazed, she sucked an ice-cube. 'What did your father say!'

He shrugged. 'I can't remember. Anyway, what's so urgent that you had to drag me out?'

Now she had the chance, she didn't know how to start. 'I was talking to Sandy. She's worried about you.'

Mick laughed, a hollow sound. 'I'm surprised she even thinks about me. She's got Anna, hasn't she?'

'That's not fair.' Katie pulled an orange plait round and chewed it. 'They never see you. You're getting obsessed with this Rowan.'

He stared at her, astonished. 'What?'

'You heard. And you're playing too much. It's not good for you.'

'Rubbish.' He looked as if he was going to get up and walk away so she said, 'You wouldn't say that if you knew Alex.'

'Alex?'

'I told you about him. He's . . . Look Mick, he says you're in danger. From that woman.'

Mick was watching her, his eyes bright in a new

way. 'I think you'd better tell me what you mean,' he muttered.

She told him Alex's story. To her surprise he listened intently, pulling long stalks out of the hay bale and bending them into circles and spirals. Feeling silly, she told him about the strange episode at the burial chamber. 'He's not right. He was standing there talking to air. So I don't believe all this stuff about Rowan . . . but, well, I'm just telling you because . . .' she shrugged, wondering why she was.

Mick chewed straw. 'You think I'll end up as cracked as him.'

'It's just that it's so similar.'

'He said this woman was Rowan?'

'Not at first. Then he did. Daft, isn't it.'

'I like her. I've never been happier.' He said it quickly, as if he was defiant.

She nodded, hiding her surprise. 'Just make it up with your Dad.'

'Katie McBride. Agony aunt.'

They both giggled.

'Tell Rowan you won't be playing so much,' Katie said firmly.

'I can't.'

'Why? You're not scared of her, are you?'

He glared angrily. 'Of course not!'

'Then tell her.'

'All right!' He stood up, facing away. 'I will. The trouble is, you don't know what it's like.' He swung round, and she saw the weariness in him. 'They've taught me so much. The music doesn't stop, it's wonderful Katie. I don't want to lose it.'

'You won't.' Uneasy, she watched him. 'Just take it easier. Promise?'

He was silent. Then he said, 'Promise.'

Instantly, a hum gathered in the air, rising to a pitch as if a hive of angry bees had overturned. All at once it was everywhere, so that Katie clapped her hands over her ears, and every microphone on the Field roared and hissed with it.

'What is that?' she yelled.

Mick shook his head. The hum tormented him; he protected his head as if to keep it off but it thrummed deep as pain so all his nerves and stomach and brain were a shuddering sickness, and when it stopped, suddenly, he was almost at screaming point.

Cautious, Katie lowered her hands. 'It's got to be that PA system.'

She looked round at the stunned tourists. A baby was screaming, dogs barking wildly. Out of sight the drums still thudded.

'Unless . . .' she giggled.

'What?'

'Unless that's what makes the crop circles.'

'That was me,' he said quietly.

'You!' After a moment she grinned. 'Idiot. I almost believed you then.'

Mick smiled too. A cold, frightened smile.

TWELVE

I am overpowered by a force which is greater than my counsel, which is greater than my strength . . .
ADVENTURE OF CONLE.

He ate the spaghetti without tasting it, winding it endlessly round his fork.

Sandy smiled over the baby on her lap. 'I can never do that, either.'

It was hot in the flat. All the windows were open; no breath of air stirred the curtains. Looking out he saw the trees beyond the still lake, black as a threat.

Putting the fork down, he stood up. It was seven o'clock. 'I think I'll go and listen to some tapes.'

Sandy looked sadly at the half-full plate. 'Your Dad will be home soon. Maybe you could both go to the Leisure Centre. Badminton, or swimming. It would do you both good to get away for a bit.'

Mick shrugged. 'If he wants.'

He went and dumped the plate on the draining board and behind him Sandy said, 'How did you two get on, Mick, before I came?'

He turned in surprise. 'Fine. But it's not you.'

'Are you sure?' She pulled the long strands of blonde hair from her cheek. 'Because if I thought it was . . .'

'It's nothing to do with you.' He leaned back against

the sink, concerned. 'Honestly. Dad and I still get on all right, I suppose, underneath. But he never wanted me to do music, right from the start, and he hates the Fair. I don't know why. I mean, I know it's extra work for him, but it seems more than that.'

'Perhaps he's jealous.' She said it softly, looking up at him with her mischievous eyes.

Mick was puzzled. 'Of what?'

'The people. Travellers, musicians, craftsmen. Their freedom.'

'He hates all that.'

'Does he?' She smoothed the baby's head. 'Did you know he wanted to be an archaeologist when he was your age?'

'*Dad*?' Mick was staggered.

'Even old fogeys were young once.'

'He never told me.' It hurt him, he realised.

'No.' She shook her head. 'I think he'd forgotten himself, till recently.'

Mick wandered to the door.

'Shall I tell him you'll go out?' she asked.

Uncertain, he paused halfway through. Then he said 'OK.'

First though, he'd have to tell Rowan.

Lying on his bed, he watched the wind-chimes. There was no wind, not even a breeze, but still they swayed, softly jangling, as if in the air of some other country, the one in all the folk songs, over the hills and far away. The notes were sweet and delicate, but none of them satisfied him, none of them were the chime of the Branch, that breathtaking sound he was always listening for now.

Outside, the moon's edge was silver over the trees.

He sat up, picked up the flute, and went out.

Stokesey Hall was dark and cavernous. He wandered along its corridors, under the flat framed faces of the long-dead, through the State rooms, down the servants' backstair, opening the hidden door in the panelling, out on to the landing above the Great Stair. He leaned over the ornate bannister in the moonlight, listening.

Below, somewhere, they were playing.

The music was plaintive tonight; one sole piper fingering a lament, the long chords shivering and chilling his spine even from here. Faintly the sound drifted along the dusty passageways.

They had been in the house for days, as if he had somehow let them in. He wasn't sure how.

Quietly, Mick padded down the stairs, the soft carpet springy underfoot. At the bottom he stepped over the red tasselled rope and edged between still shapes of furniture; a *chaise longue*, the small table with the gilt clock, the writing desk where a half-written letter always lay. As if the owners had just gone out, his father would say.

He opened the double doors to the Cedar Room.

The music was louder in here. Through tall unshuttered windows rectangles of moonlight slanted, silvering the fat whiskered faces carved among clustered foliage.

The room was wide and empty; walking across the creaky floor he felt small and breathless, a deep subdued excitement throbbing through him. Fingers on the cold brass handle, he waited.

The lament moaned with sorrow; all the pain of the world was expressed in it. He turned the ring and went in.

They were there.

All around the room, silent on windowsills, sprawled on the floor on chairs and mantelshelf and tabletop, the Midnight Court watched him with their narrow, glinting eyes.

The Gilt Room had lost all colour. It was silver, its splendour drained to a cold shining. The pipes he could hear were Irish; a small girl was playing them, her long fingers touching the holes delicately. Her face was beautiful, but when she stopped playing and smiled at him he knew she was old, older than the house, older than he could dream.

'Mick!'

Rowan was sitting on a windowsill, full in the moonlight. The small crescents in her ears dangled and glinted. He went over to her, suddenly glad.

'We've been waiting for you.' She caressed his hair lazily. 'We're all going to the Eilder Field. You'll never have heard such music.'

He glanced away. 'Thanks. But if you don't mind, just for tonight, I won't come.'

She said nothing. No one did. Suddenly he felt the moonlight was chill.

'I thought I'd go out with my father. For a change.'

A low hiss rose from a dark corner. Rowan slid off the sill and stood up, so close to him that he backed away.

'Not come?' she whispered, ominously quiet.

Mick's heart was thudding, his palms wet. With a

97

sickening shock he realised Katie had been right. He was afraid of her.

'Just this once.' He stammered, tried to smile. 'I'll be back tomorrow.'

The creatures watched him, silent. There seemed more of them than before; dim shapes in corners, forms slithering in through the open windows.

Rowan shook her head. 'I'm disappointed,' she said drily. 'Who have you been talking to, Mick?'

He didn't want to answer; it was as if the word was forced out of him. 'Katie.'

'That little cat.' Rowan watched him narrowly, her head tilted. 'And what did she have to say?'

'Nothing. At least . . . Well it was some story about a harper. Called Alex.'

At the name, the hiss spat all around the room; someone laughed, a harsh yowl like a fox's.

'It would be better not to say his name.' Rowan was cold with fury, her eyes narrow and hostile. 'So you want to do as he did, do you? You want to leave us.'

'No! I don't!'

'Listen to me Mick, no one escapes from us. The music is in you, our gift. Shall we take it back?'

'No . . . Look . . .'

'We can take it. As easily as we gave it.'

He felt ashamed, wanted to argue, but couldn't.

'Go to your father. We won't stop you.'

'I don't want to.' He looked up, said it louder. 'Not any more.'

'Then play.' She smiled, a cold amused smile that struck fear right through him. 'Go on, Mick. Play for us here. Find out how we punish those who try to get away.'

He felt hot, confused. He didn't want to play, but his fingers seemed to work despite himself, fumbling the cold tube of the flute against his lips.

A few strong arms hoisted him on to the table.

And then, unwillingly, before he knew it, he was playing, a fast, breathless reel that he didn't even recognise, the crowd roaring with laughter, dancing round him over the floor, and there were other instruments too, joining in, a whole band rampaging in every corner of the room.

Tall among her people, Rowan smiled up at him. 'Stop when you're tired Mick,' she mocked. 'Any time you like.'

But he couldn't stop. Faster and faster the music was dragged out of him; it roared on and he had to keep up with it, his fingers stabbing over the stops, his breath snatched, the pain in his chest growing like a balloon that might suddenly burst. Terrified, he couldn't see now, only blurs of giggling faces thrust up to him, leaping away. Sweat ran in his eyes and he closed them and played, and every time he thought the jig would end it switched effortlessly into another, and another, till he screamed silently with all his soul for it to stop. The rhythm drove him on, relentless; drums and pipes and voices roaring all round him, and his fingertips were so sore they bled and he couldn't breathe, he couldn't, he could feel himself suffocating, the music stifling him as he played and played, on his knees now, with Apollo watching in concern, and Rowan dancing, and dark birds or blotches swooping behind his eyelids and the stabbing in his chest sharp as knives.

The room throbbed to darkness, an agony of sound; he knew he would die of it, that they were killing him with music, and then someone came in and put the light on and his father said, 'Michael?'

He collapsed.

On hands and knees he crumpled on to the table, gasping for air, dragging it in, retching with pain and dizziness, feeling his father's hands grab him and hold him steady.

The flute rolled over the dark mahogany and clattered to the floor. Outside the room lightning flickered, like laughter.

THIRTEEN

He went his way homeward
with one star awake.
As the swan in the evening
moves over the lake.

TRAD.

Watching the news in the caravan, Katie heard the thunder. She came out on to the steps. 'Is that a storm?'

Her mother was plucking dried washing off a hawthorn bush.

'Feels like it. It's been threatening all day.'

A silent flash made Katie jump. For a second she'd seen the whole caravan field, brilliantly white.

Then, after a hush, the thunder rolled; a long, long, crumpling rumble, so deep it seemed a heaviness just over her head. The hot evening was sultry with cloud, an angry mass of greyness piling up over the Field.

'Get everything in,' her mother sighed.

They crammed chairs and table and cushions into the van. Then Katie grabbed her waterproof. 'I'll go and help Dad.'

'You be careful,' her mother muttered. 'Keep out from the trees.'

Katie went out, racing along to Frobisher's van. Martin was sitting on the steps, smoking, watching the sky.

'Will it rain?' she asked, turning and walking backwards.

'More than that.' He looked so worried she stopped. 'What do you mean?'

He didn't answer. Instead he stubbed the cigarette out on the step and said, 'Earth-lights. Corn circles. Now this witch-brew. The Fair is infested, Katie.'

She smiled and went on, but the sombreness of his voice had scared her; it hadn't been a joke.

Another flicker, its silence unnerving.

She came round the wood, picking her way in the growing dimness through nettles and ran on to the Field just as the first great drops of rain pattered on her hood. It came slowly at first, then in seconds the downpour was torrential, a crashing curtain all over her, the Field lost in it, so that suddenly the night stank of rain and rotten things, and the sulpherous crackle of electricity.

She tried to get her breath, but already the water ran in streams down her neck, soaking her hair.

She ran on.

Stalls loomed up, canvases sagging. One loose flap torn from its peg fluttered wildly in the rising wind. When she got to it the forge was empty; all the candlesticks and ironware stacked safely under sacking. There was no sign of her father.

Overhead the thunder rolled again, the gale roaring in the tops of the wood. She couldn't believe it had been hot and still an hour ago.

Trapped by the rain pouring from the roof, she crouched in the entrance, shivering. People were shouting out there; she saw a few blurred figures moving dimly, but she could almost believe the Fair was gone, spirited away, the night empty.

Lightning flickered, a sudden flaring bolt that made

all her skin prickle; sparks leapt from the commentary box, and for an incredible second she saw all its cables were scorching blue snakes, lashing in torment.

'Sand!' somebody yelled. 'Get the sand!'

She raced out to help them, and staggered sideways in the raging wind. Dizzy, she was flung against something hard; her hands told her it was one of the oaks in the centre of the field, its branches moaning in the gale, small twigs whipping past her. She'd lost all direction, crouching down, the rain battering her.

Underfoot, the ground was soft; trickles of water pouring across it. The wind howled and raged. Lifting her head she saw across the black Field tentpoles and posts torn up, canvas edges flapping, every rope snatched out by the storm. Figures in oilskins were struggling to hammer them down; near her some canvas not secured tore suddenly and harshly, ripped wide, so that the screaming wind swooped inside, rampaging, flinging everything out.

Objects gusted past Katie as she clung to the tree; paper cups, straw, leaflets, crisp packets, a silk scarf that plastered its sodden blue beauty against the wide trunk. She peeled it off, cramming it in a pocket. In the craft marquee the stalls were shattering, the crash of wooden furniture mingled with a bizarre scent of pot-pourri, and then that was flying all about her, a fragrant rain of petals and peel, stinging her face, whirled instantly away.

Still the rain came in torrents, fast as spears across the gloomy field, running down the tree-trunk over her cold fingers, the oak branches splintering and cracking above her, as if a host of invisible tormentors trampled it heartlessly.

And suddenly she saw how fragile the Fair was; a ramshackle mushroom structure that sprouted only for a fortnight, all frail canvas and thin poles, whirled away easily; there was nowhere solid here to hide, no protection, all of her world crumpling and collapsing round her.

It scared her. She had always thought of it as firm and real, a beacon of her year, but maybe it wasn't, any of it, all the life they were leading, the musicians and storytellers and poets, maybe all their art was as insecure as this, breakable, blasted away by the contemptuous gales.

Above, a thrashing branch snapped with a fierce crack.

'Katie!'

The yell came from her left; looking over she could just see Alex, crouched in the lee of the story tent. Taking a deep breath she ran, struggling through the drenching rain, hearing the branch crash behind her with a springing and snapping of endless twigs. She flung herself in beside him.

'It's incredible! Where did all this come from!'

'From them.' His words were so quiet she barely heard them over the screaming gale, but they chilled her. Silent, she looked at him.

He wore a wax coat, streaming with rain, his long hair soaked, pushed back. The rucksack lay beside him. She realised it was fully packed.

'You're going?' she whispered.

The wind roared against them, flinging over the dough-nut stand opposite with a deafening clatter. Instinctively they crouched lower, debris hurtling past them.

She caught his sleeve. 'Don't, Alex. Stay with us.'

'They're angry,' he yelled. His voice was bleaker than she'd ever heard it. 'This is their doing, Katie. You don't realize how destructive they can be; they don't care!' He twisted round and looked at her. 'What did Mick do?'

'Mick! I don't know.'

'Did you warn him? Is that it? Did you tell him about me?'

Confused, she nodded, then yelled 'yes,' the word half lost in the screech of the gale.

Alex cowered, his arm up to protect his head. Twigs pattered against them, the whole Field bending under the storm that howled and cried in eerie voices through the streaming clouds.

'He's defied her,' he muttered, almost to himself. The rain dripped from his soaked hair.

'Then stay!' Katie yelled. 'If you think he's in danger you've got to help him!'

'I can't!' He glanced at her, his eyes dark and terrified. 'She's too strong for me. I can't. Just . . . don't let him go with her.'

'Go with her!' Alarmed she dragged the soaked orange hair from her eyes. 'Go where?'

'Away. Another place.' Seeing her astonishment he seemed to make a great effort to explain, his voice almost angry. 'She'll try to entice him away, maybe at Lammas; promise him all kinds of things. You've got to keep him here! If he goes, Katie, he'll never come back! It's up to you; he won't want to listen to you though, he'll be desperate to go with them. He'll hate you, threaten you, he won't know what he's saying, but for God's sake don't let him go!'

She had never seen him so firm; then it was gone, and the old fears and uncertainties crept back over him like a shadow. He shook his head in despair.

'Don't look at me like that. You don't have to tell me I'm a coward.'

Suddenly she was frightened, and furious with him. 'Running away is useless! Help us! You understand this. I don't.'

'I can't.'

'You can! You have to think of Mick!'

'No. You don't understand.' He was scrambling up now, tugging away from her. Rain lashed between them, the wind forcing her back as if it was something alive.'

'Alex!'

'Take this.' He crammed something cold into her soaked hands; she grabbed at it as it slipped, afraid the wind would snatch it away.

'Goodbye, Katie,' he yelled, swinging up the rucksack.

'Where will you go?' she asked bleakly.

'Anywhere. Away from this.' He stood a moment looking into the storm, then he was out, running hard into the rising gale.

'We need you, Alex!' she screamed, but the words were drowned in rain, and already he was lost, a shadow in the grey veils of water.

The wind roared and whined and raged, whipping out her hair, screaming its anger. She crouched and opened her hand. In the darkness she could barely see what was in it, but even before she felt it carefully with numb fingers she knew what he'd given her. The iron disc.

A sudden crash of lightning snatched her breath; looking up she saw Stokesey Hall, its downstairs windows all flickering with blue light.

'Mick!' she breathed, furiously. 'What have you done?'

Jumping up, she raced towards it through the rain.

FOURTEEN

Westron wynde, when wilt thou blow?
The small raine down can raine.

TRAD.

'Beats me how you can sleep with all these things jangling.' His father spun one of the wind-chimes and frowned. 'There must be more than a dozen. Why so many?'

'I like them.'

Mick climbed into bed and lay back wearily on the pillow. Sandy perched by him anxiously. 'Are you sure you feel all right now?'

'I told you. I'm fine.'

He saw them exchange a glance. Outside the storm rumbled, the rain pelting the windows as if to batter its way in. He felt sick and dizzy and so tired he just wanted to sleep, but even now they didn't go.

'I still don't see why you were up on the table.' Mr Carter said stubbornly.

'I told you! I just . . . was. I was playing the flute and had a sort of dizzy spell. That's all.'

'It was a lot more than that.'

'I was breathless. It must have been the heat. I'm fine now. At least, I would be, if you'd let me get some sleep!' He made an effort and smiled, but the flicker of lightning lit their anxious faces, and suddenly it was all too much. 'Please?' he moaned.

Sandy stood up. 'Come on Mike. He's right.'

She came round and bent to brush the hair off his forehead; he jerked back, thinking of Rowan.

'Touchy! Now if you feel ill again you yell, Mick. Any time.'

'I will.'

Thunder rolled. His father crossed to the round window, looking out in concern. Then he closed the curtains. Behind the rattle of the rain, Mick heard the thin voice of the wind screaming like a banshee. He shuddered, curling himself up against the sick fear in his stomach, the chill of his clenched hands.

'I'll have to get over there. The Fair will take a bit of damage.' His father looked at Sandy. 'Will you be all right?'

'Of course. Just don't get fried by some thunderbolt.'

Mr Carter crossed the room. 'Goodnight Mick. Go to sleep.'

'Goodnight,' he whispered.

They went out. He was alone, in the dark.

For a long time he lay like that, clenched, a tight knot of fear. He was exhausted but he couldn't relax. Twice he sat up, looking all around, afraid she was here.

Slowly, warmth crept into him, but all his mind would do was replay the horror and the betrayal of the endless music, and even now his fingers twitched, his lips were dry and sore. How could she have done that to him? What else would she do?

He curled and uncurled under the sheets, sweating as the lightning glimmered through the join in the curtains. How could he ever get away from her? She controlled him, through what he wanted, and yet there had to be a way, there had to be. Alex had done it. He tried to remember what Katie had said about the harper – about some illness, the hospital. Was this what they had done to him? Was this only the beginning? The vision of some terrible pursuit flickered through his mind like the lightning; he squashed it in terror, rolling up, turning over.

The room was black. In the high rafters things shifted; sweating, he stared up at them but all he could see was dust disturbed by the draughts, drifting in strange shapes. At the bed's foot the wind-chimes jangled, a soft, endless murmur.

She would come. He knew that. He lay in an agony of listening. The great house creaked and moved as the storm raged, rattling distant windows and howling round the gables, each sound catching at his heart with cold fingers. The house wasn't his any more. All the dark corridors below him, the rooms and stairways and halls, were enemy-held; they were haunted with invisible murmurs and laughter. Once he was sure he heard music, a low, sly whistling that made his whole body clench again in dread. But the roar of the storm drowned it out, and he pulled the duvet over his head and prayed that the wind would rage for ever, that the house would never be quiet again.

He might have dozed.

But all at once he was awake, and the fear was inside him.

It came without warning. In the warm dark he stiffened till he was hot and breathless. Pushing the duvet back, little by little, he opened his eyes.

At his back, the room was still. All he could see

was the door, and that was closed.

He edged himself up on the pillow, gazing fearfully into the familiar shadows, making out the wardrobe, the shelves, the table at the end of the room.

Lightning glimmered, white and silent.

He saw her.

Terror shivered through him. It had only been for an instant, but she had been there, sitting in the old armchair against the wall, watching him. The after image dazzled him; then in the dark he thought he made out her shape, still there, unmoving.

'Rowan?' he breathed.

For a second he wasn't sure. Until, with a swiftness that made his heart lurch, she stood up and walked towards him through the dimness, her dress rustling behind her.

She sat on the bed, where Sandy had been. Still in the dark he couldn't read her face, it was so cold.

'I'm sorry, Mick.' Her voice was quiet.

'Sorry?' He was astonished.

'For all that. You must hate us.'

'No,' he stammered, confused. 'No, I don't.'

She shook her head. 'I had to do it; you shouldn't have defied me. But I want you with us. Don't you want that too?'

Numb, he shrugged. It was terrifying how she could change her mood. He saw now she was wearing a red dress, seventeenth century – he recognized it from one of the portraits downstairs. It looked odd with her short hair.

She raised an eyebrow. 'Does that mean no?'

'No,' he said hastily. 'I mean . . . yes. I want to.'

'Good. So we can be friends again.'

In a flicker of lightning her eyes were very bright.

'Did you bring the storm?' he whispered. 'Because of me?'

She smiled, faintly. 'How could I do that?'

'Don't make fun of me,' he muttered.

That annoyed her. 'You still haven't learned.' Leaning forward her voice turned cold and brisk. 'I'm fond of you, Mick, but once you take our gifts we have the right to ask for payment. Fear us, don't trust us, because we can't be trusted. We're changeable as the wind. We have no hearts. But we have everything else you can dream of.'

With a rustle of silk she stood up, crossed to the window and opened it. The wind roared in, sending the chimes jangling in an instant cacophony, chilling him with flung rain. Instantly he thought of the harvest, miles of ruined crop.

Rowan turned, her elbows on the sill. No drops stained her dress. 'Are you coming then?'

'Where?'

'I told you. Tonight we play on the Eilder Field. The storm won't bother us. Get dressed Mick. We need all our musicians.

It was an order. He knew he dared not disobey her.

After a moment he swung his feet out of bed.

His body felt cold, as if something human had left it.

Katie slammed against the flagpole for the third time and screamed with frustration. Behind her, they giggled, and she turned instantly, but the night was a roaring emptiness.

They were leading her in circles. Every time she ran

towards the Hall the wind shoved her away, the rain blinded her.

'Leave me alone!' she yelled, then dragged the iron disc from her pocket, pulling the icy wet chain over her soaked hair. Then she tried again, running hard.

This time she made it to the gate.

Jumping over it, impatient, she saw how the Hall was crawling with lights. Blue and small they rippled in all the downstairs windows, tiny globes appearing and winking out in the dark rooms. Some were out on the lawn; they drifted towards her. Ignoring them, she raced over the soaked grass between the beds of wind-flattened flowers.

Mick's window was dark, but open, the curtains billowing in.

'Mick!' she yelled.

Half way down the Great Stairs he heard her, the call making his head jerk up. 'What was that?'

'Nothing.' Smoothly, Rowan came down and rustled past him. 'Getting nervous, Mick.'

She led him under the portraits, looking like some figure that had stepped out of its frame. They crossed the South Hall and she unbolted the door, filaments of cobweb drifting in the disturbed air. Looking back, Mick saw the silent globes of light, down the corridors, in all the rooms.

When the door opened, she ushered him through, one hand on his back. They left it wide. Coming down the steps, there was no storm. He walked on wet grass on a calm night, and above him the moon hung, an owl flitting soundlessly across it. Worlds away, a wild wind blew.

★　★　★

112

'Mick!'

As soon as she saw him Katie fought her way through the gale running over the grass. Then she stopped, breathless. He didn't look up, or even seem to see her.

She turned on Rowan in fury. 'What have you done to him? Let him go!'

The woman smiled, her eyes sharp, her voice lazy. 'Why should I?'

'Why can't he see me?'

'He doesn't want to. Go home, girl. Let him be.'

'No!' Pushing past her, Katie grabbed Mick's sleeve and felt nothing but rain, her fingers passing right through him.

'Mick!' she yelled desperately, in terror.

Abruptly, he looked up. Rowan was laughing.

'Katie? Where did you come from?'

'Are you all right?'

'I'm fine,' he said, rubbing his face with one hand.

'Look, you don't have to go with her . . .'

'I do.'

'Is . . .'

'I want to go.' He looked straight at her, and his voice was cold, his face as white as if moonlight lit it. 'I have to. Stay out of this Katie, none of it's your business.'

Afraid, she whispered. 'Is she making you?'

For a second he was silent. Then he said 'No. I really want to.'

He meant it.

Stunned, sick with despair she watched them walk away through the rain. Then she saw the earth-lights were closing in on her. They were glowing stones now, carried by children, a ring of beautiful blonde children of about eight, their faces thin-lipped, all round her.

She backed off, gravel crunching underfoot.

The children came after her. One giggled, showing sharp teeth.

The first stone struck her on the face; she gasped, putting her hand to the sudden bloody scratch. Then others were hailing down on her, sharp blue sparks, the children laughing and screeching.

'Mick!' she screamed.'Mick!' but he was walking away with Rowan, and he never looked back, not once, and she was screaming and stumbling back with her arms over her head, till the hard edge of something cold thumped her in the back and she crumpled and curled, waiting for the next blow.

Nothing came.

She lay there a long minute. Then, looking out through her hair she saw the lawns were dark and empty in the falling rain. Stiff, she sat up, pulling out a tissue and mopping her cheek with it. Blood ran down, dripping. Her shoulders and arms were sore with bruises. Her hands shook; she muttered a few furious, hopeless swear words.

Glancing up, she saw that she had backed into the Fountain of Apollo. The young god gazed down at her, his curly hair running water, his hand frozen in a silent music on the strings of the lyre. In the pool raindrops pelted.

Far off, in a lull of the wind, she heard music on the Eilder Field, a drum that had begun to beat.

'They've got Mick,' she hissed up at him. 'And I don't know what to do.'

114

PART THREE

The Corn King

FIFTEEN

She turned about her milk-white steed
And took True Thomas up behind,
And aye whene'er bridle rang
The steed flew swifter than the wind.

TRAD.

Mick lay in the afternoon sun. Above him, light flecked the leaves of the oak.

Far off, faint as a dream, came the sawing and hammering, the repairing of the smashed Field. Across the meadow, the cornfields stirred in their soft music.

'Tell me again,' he murmured sleepily.

Rowan put her thumbnail through the last daisy–stem and threaded it, gently. Then she dropped the crooked crown on his head.

'Corn King,' she whispered.

He blew up at it, grinning. 'It's in my eyes.'

She twitched it straight.

'In the Land of the Young' she said quietly 'there is no rain, no sadness, no pain. Fruit and flowers grow on the trees; summer is eternal there, eternally warm. Everyone has all they need. No one needs to work.'

'That's the best bit.'

She smiled down at him. 'And my house, Mick. It stands on the cliff, overlooking the sea. Pillars of white bronze, soft hangings and music, music all the

117

time, because there is no time, and through the open windows the woods full of singing birds. No one dies; no one grows old. No one is lonely.'

He was silent, his eyes closed. Then he rolled over and looked up at her. 'I wish it existed.'

'It exists. Your Fair is just an echo of it. For those who pay the price, it may be the realest place they'll ever know.' She leaned back on her elbows. Today she wore jeans, like Katie.

'You see Mick, it's what all artists and musicians really want, even if they don't know it themselves. To step out of the world. I should know.' She laughed quietly, remembering. 'I've known so many of them down the ages. Thomas and Tam Lin, Taliesin, Conle, Oisin. None of them could resist it.'

He watched her. As always, the things she said confused him, almost hypnotized him. Vaguely he knew he was losing himself, but it didn't matter so much now. Since the storm, two nights ago, they had never left him alone; in his room, in the Hall, in the sessions and dances on the Field, some of them were always there, always talking to him. It didn't bother him any more, he thought. He'd been stupid to be afraid of them. They might hurt him, you never knew what they'd do, but this was his chance, his one chance to be the best, to be different to all the others. To step out of the world.

Rowan tapped him with a daisy. 'You're tired,' she said. 'Close your eyes.'

He obeyed, turning over and stretching out on the grass, seeing nothing but a red heat that drifted under his eyelids, and as he lay there the weight of the July sun warmed his face and neck. Her voice tickled him, close as a whisper.

'Go to sleep.'

They were riding on a white horse. Gradually he realised that, and he knew they had been riding for hours, for years, and that he was holding tight to Rowan in front of him, and under them was water, the green, impossible depths of the sea, white gulls screaming overhead.

They were galloping through spray and foam, the horse's hooves spume-flecked, the salt smell fresh and exhilarating. Mick's face was wet; he gave a shout of delight, so that terns rose from the rippling waves and Rowan turned and laughed at him over her shoulder.

All the world was water, a lifting surface of foam patches, and as he leaned down he saw his own face reflected, and then, with a shock, another landscape below that, far down in the depths, a whole other country drowned down there. He saw its hills and mountain ranges, green valleys where tiny sheep scattered as the horse's shadow darkened over them.

'Where is that?' he gasped, but Rowan only laughed. 'Who knows?' she called above the gulls.

There were people down there too; they came running out of their houses and farms, pointing up at him in amazement.

'Am I dreaming?' he asked, as the horse galloped over the spire of a drowned church, tiny and grey.

'Of course you are.' She was looking ahead, sharp-eyed, the small moons swinging from her ears. 'Life's a dream Mick. All of it.'

The horse ran faster, spray splashing high. Suddenly

sea mist gathered round them, a chill dampness that condensed on Mick's hair, making him shiver. As they raced through it he caught glimpses of things in the greyness: a hawk chasing a swallow, the small deft bird darting past his shoulder; and a little later a hare dashed out of the glinting fog, its eyes wide with terror, gone in seconds, with a greyhound yelping after it, almost tangling in the horses' legs. Rowan said nothing; he didn't ask.

Later, a strange rhythmic creaking made him stare up into the cloud; he saw four swans flying high, linked in pairs by gleaming silver chains, glimpsed and lost among the rags of mist. Rowan glanced up once, then urged the horse on faster, the bells on its harness rippling in the speed of their ride.

Bursting out of the clouds Mick gasped in delight, for now the sea was an endless plain of brilliant flowers, red and gold and blue, and far off to the east a fairhaired man was driving a fiery chariot across it, whipping on two black glossy horses towards a great stone keep, its pennants streaming in the wind. Rowan raised her hand and waved, and the man waved back, yelling something, his long hair tossed in the sea wind.

'Who was that?' Mick asked.

Rowan only laughed. Then she yelled 'Look ahead!'

Over the plain he saw an island, rising up. Its high peaks shone green in the sunlight; even from here he could see the oak woods that covered it, hear the singing of its myriad birds. The sweet flowers grew thinner till the horse was racing over water again, and he could see beaches of yellow sand, all the bays and coves, and on the sea cliff a great house, its walls of some strange glimmering metal, fine fabrics of silk and purple billowing from its windows.

'My house,' Rowan called, her voice triumphant.

'I see it! But who's that on the beach?'

'On the beach? Where?' Suddenly Rowan sounded alarmed.

'By that cave. Waiting for us.'

As they thundered nearer he saw her clearly. A woman with fair hair, wearing a yellow sundress just as she did in the photograph on his father's desk. For a second he had thought it was Sandy, but now, his hands prickling with fear and bitter, heart-striking longing, he knew it was his mother, his real mother, who he could never remember, who had died when he was barely two.

'*No!*' With a great hiss of anger, Rowan slewed the horse to a halt; it neighed and skidded, splashing the water in a great wave over them, so that Mick's face was soaked.

His mother sat on a rock and looked out at him. She was calm, not even smiling.

'Am I still dreaming?' he whispered, his voice cold and small.

No one answered him.

He opened his eyes. There was salt on his lips; his soaked shirt was half-dry. Sitting up slowly, he knew that the Field was dark. He was stiff and cold. Hours had passed.

From the roots of the oak tree one of the wolf-twins looked over from their game of cards.

'About time,' he growled, contemptuous.

'Action,' the director snapped.

The camera panned over the Eilder Field, over the vast flattened circles in the crop, the interlocking arcs,

121

the great spiral in the centre. Then it zoomed in on a man in a grey suit and striped tie, who began to speak rapidly at it.

'At the Great Lammas Fair at Stokesey this year, the crop circles keep on coming. Two days ago, after the storm which caused so much damage here, this one, the biggest so far, was discovered. Can this really be a hoax, and, if so, what trickster could have managed it on that stormy night? Or is it some natural manifestation? Earlier, I spoke to Dr Martin Donahue, of the Meteorology Department at Southampton University. What did he think were the origins of this mysterious phenomenon?'

'OK. I'm not sure about phenomenon.' The director peeled himself off the gate, and the man in the suit reached out and took a drippy ice-cream cone from the sound-man and ran his tongue round it. 'Can't I just take the jacket off?' he asked wearily.

Katie watched them in disgust.

'Look at them. Don't they realise this is serious!'

Tom scratched his stubbly cheek. 'Superstitious, your lot.'

She knew he meant the Fair people, and shrugged, uneasy.

'I see some have left.'

That was true too. 'Yes. The singers from Tralee went. Some of the Shetland people. A few of the stalls have packed up. It was the storm scared them off. And the rest.'

Tom looked at her closely. 'The rest, most likely. Word is that the Fair's being overrun. Lots of them, here now, gone, then back again. Fires in the Eilder Field all night.

In the morning, not even a charred stick. I know, I looked. Music, all hours; even down at my place I can hear it at nights. Tents no one's seen before. Things going wrong, going missing. And that night of the rain, someone told me there were lights, blue flickering things, all over the Hall.'

She stared out at the flattened crop, the butterflies dancing over it. 'So you believe in supernatural things, Tom?'

The groundsman gave a gruff laugh. 'When you live as long as I have, lass, you believe in more and more, not less and less. But why they've come, and who brought them, I don't know. Seems to me we should be very wary on Lammas Night.'

'Why?'

He glanced at her. 'You know why. The year has cracks. Gaps. That's when there are ways between worlds. You could fall through then, right out of the world. Lammas is one. The harvest, the turning of the year. And these people, they always come for someone.'

She wanted to say, 'They've come for Mick', but even as she thought it, Mick's father swung through the gate. 'Haven't these bloody reporters gone yet?' he fumed. He flicked through a sheaf of paper on a clipboard. 'Look, Tom, get over to the Field. Some idiot's undone all the new ropes on the craft tent.'

Tom glanced at Katie. 'Keep calm, boss.' He walked off, leaving Mr Carter glaring at the TV crew. 'How much longer?'

'Few more shots.' The director waved, chewing a pen. 'All we need.'

As he turned to go again, Katie said quietly, 'How's

123

Mick?'

Mr Carter looked down at her. 'All right. Well, he had a bit of a funny turn, to tell the truth. A few nights ago. I'm beginning to wonder if it's not asthma – all this playing doesn't help.'

'He's all right now though?'

He shuffled paper, awkwardly. 'To be honest, Katie, I'm so rushed I don't get the chance to see much of him. Everything seems to be going wrong. As if someone's out to keep me busy. He never seems to be around at meal times either. You probably see more of him.'

No I don't, she thought, watching him go. Since the storm, Rowan's people had never left Mick alone. Wherever he was, they were there too; the wolf-twins, the tall sly one, the threatening children. He was thin, more drawn each day. Katie had barely managed a word with him. They were feeding on him, and no one else even seemed to be noticing.

She kicked the gate grimly. She had no plan, no one to tell her what to do. What if they took him, snatched him through the crack of Lammas Night, into the dark, and she'd done nothing to stop it! If only Alex had stayed! He knew about this; she had no ideas.

Chilled in the afternoon sun, she turned the disc in her fingers; it gleamed and glinted in the sun.

She had to try again. Somehow.

'Action!' the director called.

SIXTEEN

I love my love and well she knows
I love the ground wereon she goes.
If her no more on earth I see
How can I serve her as she's served me?

TRAD.

Sandy put the brake on the pushchair, and peered doubtfully into the stall. The smell of herbs was rich and strong; she saw fragrant smoke rising from some incense-burner at the back. In all the corners, faces seemed to watch her, carved in mirrors and candles.

'Hello?' she called quietly. 'Anyone in?'

The wind-chimes jangled, a soft ominous warning. So this was where Mick got them. Looking at them she thought they were tawdry; rough scraps of metal and twisted wood, but then as the sound came again she wondered how the dimness could have deceived her, because now they were finely engraved, expensive, elegant shapes, some of silver, their chimes light and graceful.

A curtain twitched. A small, ugly man sidled through, his head bald, his bright eyes hooded. He wore a red neckerchief and a Morris man's coat, all sewn with ragged strips of cloth.

He grinned at her. 'You want to buy something?'

'No.' Sandy stared at him. 'I'm looking for Mick. Someone said he'd be here.'

'Mick?' He spat the name back at her.

'Mick Carter.'

The man smirked. 'I know. Her new little mortal. I'll see.'

He went so quickly that she thought he'd disappeared. The stall made her uneasy; its sweet smells of joss and oils, the corners hung with dark cloth, glinting with tiny moons. She pushed the baby further out, into the sun, noticing how the familiar sounds of the Fair seemed louder out here.

'Mick's not here.'

A woman was leaning against the tentpole, tall and red-haired. Sandy stared at her. She had thought Rowan would be older, but this was hardly more than a girl, her face clear and unlined.

'Someone told me he would be.'

'He's not.' Rowan came out; she wore a long green dress, her feet bare. 'He might be at the sessions.'

Her eyes were green too, bright and sharp. Sandy felt as if the woman was mocking her.

'I'll try there, then.' She clicked the brake off the pushchair; Anna gurgled. 'If you see him, will you tell him to come home for supper?'

'If I see him.' Rowan glanced down at the baby. 'She's pretty. Is that his sister?'

She came and bent over the pushchair. Sandy had a sudden unreasoning surge of anxiety; she wanted to tug the baby out and hold her tight. Instead she said, 'Her name's Anna.'

'You shouldn't be so free with names.' Rowan looked up. 'Names are power.' She smiled, curious. 'Tell me, how does he feel about you? Does he resent you? After all, you're not that much older than he is.'

Sandy was speechless at the woman's nerve. She flushed angrily.

'Mick and I get on fine.'

'He's told me that. I wonder if it's true.' Rowan reached up and touched a chime; it echoed softly. 'Just think about it,' she said, reasonably. 'He's had his father to himself all these years. Now you come along. He must feel out in the cold.'

A chill crept over Sandy's heart. All at once she knew it was fear; she wanted to get away, not listen to any more of this.

'I told you. We're fine.' She turned the pushchair hastily.

'And his real mother. I know he thinks about her.'

She turned, stung into fury. Rowan's eyes were laughing, missing nothing.

'Keep away from him,' Sandy whispered.

Rowan laughed. 'Ah, but he won't keep away from me. He loves the music. More than he loves you. Or even his father.'

As she hurried away, furious and scared over the trampled grass, the pushchair bumping unnoticed, Sandy stared at nothing. Behind the ice-cream stand, she stopped abruptly.

'It's not true,' she muttered to herself, bitterly. 'It's not true.'

Katie kicked the pile of horseshoes; they slid and slithered with a clatter of metal. 'What's all this?'

'Martin's idea.' Her father raised a sweaty face from the forge, his apron black with smuts. He stretched, as if his back ached.

She stared at him.

'He's nailing them all over the stalls.' Calum grinned. 'Iron, see? Keeps away the faerie folk.'

Dragging an orange plait from her face she said 'How far has he got?'

'Three along.' He touched his new earring. 'Are these things always so sore?'

'Serves you right. Too old and vain.'

She went out and walked down the row of stalls. Martin Frobisher was up a ladder outside the jewellery stall, where pendants and Celtic brooches glittered in the sun. He was hammering a horseshoe on to the tentpole, the stall owner watching anxiously.

He climbed down, took his hat, and saw Katie.

'Brought the rest?'

'No. What are you doing?'

He took her aside. 'Protection. They don't like it.'

'They?'

He shrugged. 'Heard the latest? Wheels let down on vans in the camping field. This morning someone's glued all the wooden toys together in the craft tent, and emptied every jampot and filled them with nettles. Practical jokes. But I know whose.'

She looked at him a moment, then pulled the disc off and held it out. 'What do you know about this?'

He turned it in his blunt, musician's fingers. It was small, about the size of a large coin, and one side had a cross inscribed, with a circle round it. On the other, worn smooth by fingering, was a wheel, or maybe a sun, spokes of light radiating. As he looked at it, Katie watched, hearing around them all the life and noise of the festival, so real, so normal; dogs barking, the PA distant and garbled, accordions, wandering families, shrieks from the children's playground.

He looked up. 'Is this yours?'

'It is now.'

'I'm no expert. It feels powerful to me. Some sort of talisman. Keep it on, it'll do you no harm.'

As she took it back she saw the dance stage. Behind low swags of red and green flags, a circle of men and women were clapping and stamping. They wore Greek costumes, the woman in bright headscarves. Beside them musicians played; with a shock she saw Mick.

He was sitting, eyes closed, playing the accordion. She had no idea he could play that, but his fingers moved expertly over the keyboard, and the rich, jovial music made her want to dance too, so that she smiled. The smile faded when she looked at his face.

He was white, almost bloodless. The skin was drawn over his cheekbones; dark shadows were under his eyes. He opened them a moment and looked at her, but dully, as if he didn't see her. Then he turned and was playing and laughing, a cold laugh she'd never heard from him before.

Others were there, one on fiddle, another on whistles. A thin girl and a wizened man; both Rowan's people.

When the music stopped she pushed through the crowd and ran up to him fast, not even thinking what she would do.

'Mick!'

He looked up at her. For a moment she knew he was struggling to remember. Then he said 'Katie?'

'Don't say anything. Just put this on. Put it on!' Her hands were at his neck but when he saw the disc glint in the sun he grabbed her, fought her off as if the touch of it would burn him.

'No! Stop it!'

'It won't hurt you, Mick!'

'Leave me alone!' He flung her off, jerking free.

The others closed round, ominous. She ignored them.

'I'm trying to help! To give you some protection.'

'I told you; it's not your business.' He was white with fury; stepping forward he caught hold of her arm in a tight grip. 'Leave me alone, Katie. This is what I want. You don't understand.'

She pulled away, almost in tears. 'And will you go with her, when she asks you?'

'Go?' He looked startled.

'Away. Run off. What's she promised you Mick? The Land of the Young?'

Astonished, he stared at her. 'How do you know about that!'

'It's a dream! It doesn't exist . . .'

But she was shoved back; a huge brawny man with rings in his ears forced himself between them.

'Get lost, girl,' he said, his voice a deep threat.

She was about to defy him when she found she was being dragged; a crowd of the tiny acrobats had her hands and were pulling her, but she scrambled out of their tangle furiously and turned round to yell at them.

Turning back, she saw Mick was gone.

The big man was gone too.

As if they'd vanished.

SEVENTEEN

We see everyone on all sides, and no one sees us.
                                        IRISH ANON.

'Katie said to give you this.'

His father handed him a note; Mick flicked it open and read it.

For God's sake Mick, I only want to talk to you! Meet me at eight by the Apollo fountain. Please!
   Katie.
   PS Come on your OWN.

With a wry smile he crumpled it up, and shoved it in his pocket. Poor Katie.

'What are you looking for?' he asked his father idly.

Mr Carter slammed the drawer. 'I can't seem to find anything these days!'

Mick grinned. As his father bent down again, the small man with the wizened face sitting on top of the filing cabinet had reached down and stirred the papers on the desk. Half of them drifted to the floor. Mr Carter swore. 'Close that blasted window.'

Mick did, laughing to himself.

There were four of them in the room. No one else could see them but him. They didn't seem to have names; they rarely spoke. But he wasn't scared of them any more.

131

'Here it is!' His father stood up with a computer printout. 'Programme for Lammas Night. Running order for the closing concert. And the Ritual; though that's the same every year. I need people to play the parts though. Fancy being the Corn King?'

The mention of Lammas made Mick feel cold. Rowan had said that was the night she was leaving. She wanted him to come with her, to what she called the Land of the Young, but he wasn't sure what she meant; she was always teasing him. Some other Fair maybe, living on the road, being a musician. And why shouldn't he go? If it didn't work out he could come back; he could phone them sometimes, they wouldn't worry. They had Anna.

His father gathered up papers, knocking a small photo over, and before the wizened goblin could catch his hand, Mick had picked it up and turned it over.

His mother looked out at him. She was sitting on a green bank, hands clasped around her knees, smiling. The yellow sundress was old-fashioned and faded. For a moment he knew quite clearly that all the things he had just been telling himself were lies; knew that he was in danger, a terrible, immortal danger he barely understood. Then his father took the frame from him gently and looked at it.

'I think we ought to have a talk soon, Mick. About next term.'

Far off on the Lammas Field a drum began, beating steadily. The invisible girl by the window looked up, her eyes bright.

Mick shook his head, as if to clear it. 'What?'

'Maybe when the Fair's over, and I've got more time.'

'You mean you'll let me take music?'

132

'I didn't . . . Well, we need to look at all the options, don't we? Take your time.'

'I don't need to. I've decided.' He stood up and went out quickly, the drumming in his wrists now and in his chest.

Michael Carter stared after him. He felt guilty. Mick was looking pale. They should go out somewhere; he'd have to make time. All four of them, like a proper family. He put the photo of his first wife down and smiled at it ruefully.

'You'd know how to handle this,' he muttered.

A gust of wind raised the papers, and the frame would have toppled with a crash if he hadn't grabbed it. He glared at the closed window.

Out in the corridor, someone laughed.

There was a concert on in the main marquee; even from here Katie could hear the deep thump of the electric bass. The gardens were darkening; the first moths coming out. She shivered and wished she'd brought a pullover. Then the stable clock chimed the quarters, and she knew it was half past eight.

'You scum, Mick,' she whispered. 'Too scared even to talk to me.'

She knew he was in the Hall. High in the dim building there was a light in his room, and she'd heard the flute earlier, soft and strange, playing an old folk-tune she knew from the edges of her memory.

She got up, pacing up and down under the silent fountain. Apollo gazed down at her as she stopped.

'I'm going in,' she told him. 'After all, they can't be in the house with him.'

She turned and ran lightly over the dim lawns, jumping the corner of the floral bed and racing up the steps to the terrace. It was quieter here; the corner of the house cut off the thump of the Fair. She went through the gate to the door marked '*Private*' and pushed it, gently. It was locked.

Hissing a curse, she bit a strand of hair and turned, walking stealthily round the outside of the Hall. A few bats flitted in the early twilight. All the windows were high, out of her reach, and the main doors were locked too, as she'd known they would be, but as she came round into the cobbled courtyard at the back she saw that the servants' door was ajar, and that Mr Carter had just come out of it, and was crossing the yard with one of the technicians from the Field.

Quickly, she stepped back into the shadows.

'Sparking all over the place . . .' she heard the man mutter, and then they were gone, over the smooth grass.

In seconds she had run to the door, and slid inside.

It was dark. The corridor ran in front of her, stone-flagged. She walked down it, past the doorways of kitchens, their great spits hanging still, pewter bowls and plates laid on their vast dusty tables. At the end she stopped.

She'd been in the Hall many times, but always with Mick. Still, it wouldn't be difficult to find the way up, if she kept out of the rooms. Not many alarms, he'd said.

Something shifted behind her; she turned quickly, afraid it was Mick's father coming back, but the door was ajar, a pale slit.

She turned back.

The corridor with the bells was the one she recognised. They were coiled up there among the shadows and the cobwebs, each with the name of the room written below. As she stared up, the bell for the Satin Drawing Room tinkled, just a quiver of sound. Puzzled, she stared at it. All the visitors would have gone by now, surely?

There were more corridors than she remembered. They were all panelled and seemed the same, and she must have taken a wrong turn because she kept finding herself back at the bells, and couldn't see how. A sickening suspicion gathered in her, but she crushed it firmly, feeling the smooth disc of iron between her fingers. She'd just have to be more careful.

At the end of the next turning was a pair of closed doors. She opened them gently, and peered in.

The East Hall. She knew it from the velvet hangings. This was where the Great Stair was. At least she could go up.

Tiptoeing through the hushed masses of furniture she found the staircase and crept up it, praying that Sandy or anyone else wouldn't suddenly come down. It would be pretty awkward to explain. After all, this was like their house.

Above her on the dark walls the portraits stared down, gowned and ruffed and severe, and their eyes seemed to watch her, making her skin prickle. At the top of the second landing she felt along the panels for the handle to the hidden door; her fingers touched it, a cold ring, and turning it, the door opened. She was on the narrow servants' stair that led up to the flat. A lightbulb burned here; going up quietly she passed a window and saw the courtyard at the back, and heard distinctly the thump of the Fair. This stairway was plainer, the walls a dull cream, and the boards creaked, so she paused at the top and listened anxiously. Somewhere ahead, a television echoed; a murmur of music and voices.

135

She crept up to the door. Sandy was there, rocking the baby softly in her arms, her feet curled up on the sofa, watching some documentary about fashion.

Trying not to let the boards creak, Katie slipped by, down to Mick's room. She knew it was the one at the end.

Outside the door she wondered for a second what to do; then she tapped, gently. 'Mick?'

It was a whisper; perhaps he hadn't heard.

'Mick. It's me, Katie. Can I come in?'

For a moment she thought he wasn't there. Then footsteps crossed the floor; he had the door open and was standing inside, looking at her coldly.

'I've been waiting for you,' he said.

She came in, feeling uneasy. 'What do you mean?'

'They said you were coming up.'

Puzzled she glanced round, and her eyes widened. The room was dim, with only a lamp lit near the window, two moths fluttering wildly round it. Clustered on the ceiling like a swarm of bizarre spiders hung a host of wind-chimes, all clanging softly.

'Where did you get all those!'

He glanced up at them briefly. 'Never mind. What do you want, Katie? I wish you'd stop pestering me.'

It was hard to think, with the clink and tingle of sounds in all the shadows. 'Look, Mick,' she said, going with him to the window. 'We used to be friends.'

'Used to be is right.'

That stung her, but she just slipped the disc from her neck and held it up. 'All I want is for you to wear this. That's all. You could do that for me.'

He looked at it, suspicious. 'What is it?'

'I told you. A sort of talisman. It wouldn't hurt, under your clothes. No one would know.'

'What's it supposed to do?' he scoffed.

She shrugged, unhappy. 'I don't really know. It might make you see things differently.'

She held it out. For a moment he just looked at it, and she felt the tension rise in her, her hand shaking. He smiled, and she thought then that he'd refuse, but to her surprise he reached out and took it gently from her fingers.

Then he threw it out of the window.

'No!' she screamed. He folded his arms and laughed at her, and she shoved him aside and hung over the sill, but all the night was dark and the lawns too far below.

She turned on him in fury. 'What's the matter with you! What's happening to you!'

'I don't need your stupid lucky charms. I know what I'm doing! I'm not under some sort of spell.' He looked over her shoulder and said, 'What are we going to do with her? She's getting to be a nuisance.'

Katie's skin crawled.

The room was full, instantly, of people. With a rustle of silk someone got up from a chair just behind her and without turning she knew who it was, that they'd been here all the time.

'We'll get rid of her,' Rowan's voice said sweetly.

Mick's smile faltered. 'What do you mean?'

'Oh, not for long.' Rowan came round and stood there, leaning on the chest of drawers. 'Somewhere dark and safe. That she can't escape from. Until tomorrow night is over.'

She turned then and touched Mick's arm, and he smiled at her.

'Because after the Ritual,' she said, 'it won't matter.'

EIGHTEEN

Just at the mirk and midnight hour
The faery folk will ride.

TRAD.

Instantly, Katie was standing in some low, damp cellar.

She gasped, stifling a cry of terror.

There was no one with her but Rowan, the woman waiting with a lantern at the top of some stairs, the yellow light making her face sharp and sly. Not a woman though. A girl. A girl the same age as she was, as Mick was. Katie took a step forward.

'Where are we?' she gasped, looking round in disbelief.

Rowan smiled sweetly and put the lantern down. 'I'll leave you this. I don't know how long it will last. There's nothing to eat but I'm sure you won't starve. Someone will find you after the Ritual.' She turned.

'Wait!' Katie clenched her hands. 'You can't just leave me here!'

'Why not?'

'They'll find me before that. Someone will. When I don't come home . . .'

The girl laughed then, the small moons swinging from her ears. 'They won't even know you're missing. We can do many things, human child. One of my people will sleep in your bed, and eat your breakfast, and your parents

138

won't even know it isn't you. We've always been good at changelings.'

Cold with fear, Katie stared at her. 'You wouldn't,' she breathed.

Rowan smirked. 'I already have.'

Sandy switched the television off and stretched, wondering where Michael was. The Fair had had nothing but problems this year, and even though she'd enjoyed it, she'd be glad to see it end, for his sake. And Mick's. Mick was very, very restless.

On a whim she turned and went out into the corridor, and down to his room. Carefully she opened the door, just a slit.

'Are you awake?' she whispered.

There was no answer.

The room was dark and airy; as she opened the door wider a corruscade of notes tinkled from the ceiling. She frowned, thinking they would wake him, but there was no stir from the dark bed. The window was wide open, and she crossed over to close it, hearing the distant thump of the electric bass and nearer, other music, a soft fluting that made her pause with her hands on the catch and look down. It was coming from the lake; looking over there now she could see tiny campfires, and shadows moving round them. Who was camping there? Michael would be furious if he knew.

She decided not to tell him. He had enough to worry about. The moon was up, a pure circle shining full in her face, so that when she turned her shadow darkened the bed. She stepped aside and flooded it with light.

It was empty.

139

She stared at it in cold fright, then looked round stupidly.

'Mick?'

The wind–chimes tinkled, a silver mockery.

She could see the bathroom door; it was ajar, the room dark. He wasn't in there. Crossing the moonlight she touched the pillow and it was cold, his pyjamas bundled beneath it.

She turned, slowly, and looked out at the campfires.

Katie heard the door slam and the bolts slide. With a yell of anger she was up the steps and throwing herself on the wood, thumping with both fists. It was useless, and she was even more angry with herself for doing it. Turning, she swore, picked up the lantern, and looked round at her prison.

It seemed to be a cellar. It was very dark, the ceiling a series of arches low enough for her to touch above her head, coming down to a shadowy forest of squat pillars. It stank of damp and old wine-casks. Vast hanks of ancient cobweb festooned everything, black with centuries of grime. The floor was flagged with stone, bitterly cold.

She looked at her watch. Nine fifteen.

Warily, not sure if she was alone or not, she came down the steps and stood still. Something scuttled, not far off. Rats. That was all she needed.

Slowly, she edged forward, ducking under the webs, holding the lantern out to see where she was going. Her breath made a faint chill cloud. Twice she bumped into casks and boxes; the lid of one slithered off with a crash that sent echoes reverberating round the walls.

She waited, her heart thumping. Dust rose and settled; far ahead of her the cellars stretched into distance. She leaned over and felt inside the nearest cask; there was rope there, an ancient coil of it, and something soft and mouldy; she jerked away, quickly.

Now there were pillars all round her; there seemed to be no end to them, and she realised the underground rooms were vast, perhaps stretching under the whole of Stokesey.

If she was still in Stokesey, and not in some other dimension altogether.

'Don't be stupid,' she hissed at herself. Putting the lamp down she took a breath and yelled 'Hello!' at the top of her voice.

'I'm locked in! HELLO!'

The echoes took it and whispered it and rumbled it, but even to her it sounded pathetic. She had a sudden vision of all the empty rooms that must be above her, the corridors and stairs, all shadowy, and high and remote at the top of the house, Sandy watching television with her feet curled on the sofa.

It was hopeless.

She had to find some way out.

For an hour she wandered the pillars of the cellar, getting colder and more irritated and dirty.

And scared. Because by then she'd lost all sense of direction; pillars and casks and walls of greasy cold stone bewildered her, and when she tripped against something and found herself kneeling on the steps again, she was too exhausted and dispirited to do anything but sit in the dust and shiver.

Leaning back against the wall, she wrapped her arms

round her knees and tried to get warm. Think! she told herself, firmly.

But nothing would come, except the bitterness of Mick's scorn; the flash of that sun-disc as it had gone over the sill, his strange, cold smile. And what Rowan had said. Could they really put some creature in her place?

She knew they could. She'd known for ages now that they could do all sorts of things, and she'd been a fool not to believe Alex from the start.

If only she could find a door!

Looking at her watch again she found it was nearly midnight, and brushed the dirty hair from her eyes with bitter weariness. Tomorrow was Lammas. Tomorrow they'd take him. She had to get out of this place!

Uncoiling, she straightened. One more look round. There must be some grating she could shout through, some boarded window she'd missed.

She picked herself up and scrambled down the steps.

On the bottom one, without warning, the lamp went out.

Coming out of the concert tent with numbed ears, Calum McBride found his wife waiting for him. 'Is Katie with you?' she asked anxiously.

'No. She was probably in there though, with some of the others. Why?'

'I haven't seen her all evening.' Jean scratched her cheek thoughtfully. 'She told me she was going to see Mick.'

'Well, that's it then. She's at the Hall.'

'No I'm not. I'm here.'

142

They turned, startled. Katie grinned at them, her hair a tangle of orange. 'Scared you, did I?'

Her father frowned. 'There are a lot of strangers about this year. You know you ought to be careful.'

She shrugged, turning away. 'I know. Don't fuss.'

Martin Frobisher came up, and they all walked over the Field towards the campsite.

'Big day tomorrow,' Calum muttered.

'If it goes well.'

'Why shouldn't it? Michael Carter's a good organizer.'

'That's not what I mean.' Martin's voice was dark and sombre. 'Something's brewing. You can feel it too, so don't pretend you can't.'

'I'm just a blacksmith.' Calum smiled, uneasy. 'You musicians, you're the ones with all the sensitivity.'

His wife shook her head. 'He's right. Too many things are going wrong. People are scared.'

Martin ducked under the low branches of the trees. 'It's no wonder,' he muttered. 'Look how we live – on the edge, out of the main-stream, among old stories and songs, holding on to them, never letting them die. Folklore. Remnants of lost rites, like the Ritual. All the old half-understood beliefs. Is it any wonder they rise up and haunt us? And what's music anyway, but a sort of magic?'

Something crackled in the wood. He stopped, turned abruptly.

'Who's that?'

In the tangled thorn and hazel nothing moved, lances of moonlight sloping down between the treetrunks. An owl hooted, far over the cornfields.

'Come on,' Martin growled. 'Come out.'

For a second they thought no one would, that it was

some new trick on their senses. Then, to Martin's grim relief, they saw a man was standing there, under the nearest tree; a thin man in a dark coat, and as he moved his hair glinted pale in the moonlight.

'I'm sorry,' he said, his voice low. 'I didn't mean to startle you.'

Beside her, Mrs McBride felt Katie shiver as if in surprise.

Martin took his hat off and scratched his forehead. 'Well, well. Good to see you back, Alex.'

The harper nodded, absently. They thought he looked paler than before, nervous and edgy. 'I'd like a word with Katie,' he mumbled.

Calum looked at his wife, who shrugged. 'Don't be long.' They moved off to the nearby vans and Martin went with them, calling goodnight.

'Well.' Katie folded her arms. 'This is a surprise.'

He came up to her, grim-faced, his eyes dark in the eerie light.

'Where is she?' His voice was cold with anger.

'She?'

'Katie. What have you done with her?'

The girl giggled. 'You really need to go back to that hospital, Alex.'

He wanted to reach out and catch hold of her, but he knew it wouldn't be safe. 'You can fool them, but not me,' he said coldly. 'I was with your people far too long. I can smell sorcery even in the dark.'

She flickered then, just for an instant, merging before his eyes into a thin sly creature, long-nosed, thin-lipped, grinning. Then it was Katie, and her mother was calling her from the van steps.

'Coming!' The changeling turned back and grinned at him spitefully. 'Go and tell them, harper. Go and explain it all. I'd love to hear that.'

'Where is she?' he breathed, knowing it was hopeless.

'If the queen sees you, she'll tear out your soul.'

'I know that. Tell me where Katie is.'

It laughed at him, tangling its orange hair with one finger, bringing its face close to his ear.

'Underground,' it whispered gleefully. 'In Hell.'

NINETEEN

And aye she sat, and aye she reeled, and aye she wished for companie.

TRAD.

If the watch stopped, she'd be alone.

It had become a sort of friend, the tiny green hands the only relief from the darkness.

She had always thought darkness was just no light, but this was a living thing, thick and close like black velvet, stifling her. She couldn't believe in light any more. It would be too dazzling, too amazing. She tried to imagine it and couldn't. And the cold too, that had become a numbing pain, so deep in her bones it had been in her for ever.

When the lamp had gone out, she'd been too scared to leave the steps. If she shuffled out there into the invisible halls, groped her way between pillars and casks, how could she ever get back? It had taken her hours to think of the rope, and ages of blind groping to find it again. Tying it round her waist, she knew this was how blind people must feel.

Then she'd walked, feeling and fumbling through the great earthy spaces, shuffling into nowhere, expecting the restricting tug at any time, scared she'd run out of rope, scared it was tangled hopelessly among the pillars, scared it had untied from the barrel and was just trailing after her.

Finally, it stopped her. She didn't have the energy to feel her way back. Not yet.

She sat down, worrying, shivering. Sometimes she called out, sometimes she even slept, though whenever she woke she felt so cold she had to rub life back into her arms and limp up and down, miserable and aching. Time crept. Sometimes she looked at the green hands and they had barely moved; her heart leapt in misery, and she snatched the watch to her ear. The whisper of its tick reassured her like a voice.

Between sleep and worry, the smell of the cellars crept into her snatched dreams; an earthy smell, of worms and decay. She tried to think about Mick, about how to convince him, but what was the use? He didn't care, if Rowan asked him to go, he'd go. It was the music he wanted. She'd never realized what that meant to him, she thought, rubbing her forehead with a gritty hand. None of them had. Especially not his father. And now it was too late, because soon it would be Lammas, and she was stuck in here and no one, *no one* in the world knew.

Perhaps she slept again. Because she opened her eyes, and something had changed.

She sat upright. What was it? A sound?

Scrambling up she yelled 'Mick! Sandy! For god's sake, someone let me out!' banging on a pillar, hands flat, screaming with sudden pent-up fury.

When it was over she turned, and slid down against the stone. Silence came back, creeping out of its holes and shadows, gradually, all around her. Her eyes were wet but she swore at herself viciously, biting a thumbnail, sucking a small cut under her knuckle.

Then, she froze, hardly breathing.

That was it. She could see! She could see her hand, and the rope, and a shadow that must be some wall.

The watch said six o'clock.

Somewhere outside, far away above, the sun had come up.

It was Lammas Day.

Alex waited under the trees, cold and stiff. The sun rose slowly, magnificently through the wood, warming the palest of blue skies with its drifts of cloud. He felt the shadows shrivel, all the darkness in the corners of his mind. Lammas would be hot.

In the morning light, the facade of Stokesey Hall shone honey-bright, its tangles of wisteria buzzing with early bees. The grass of the lawns was smooth, studded with daisies, the long shadows of trees stretched across it.

He stepped out into the light, trying to warm himself.

All night he'd lain curled in the summerhouse, as far from the Field as he could get, hearing low fluting across the lake, enticing drifts of music that tore at him, but he hadn't gone, he'd stayed huddled, unable to sleep, sick with fear and longing. Now he was tired and light-headed, and he knew she was standing behind him.

'They told me you were back,' she said.

He turned.

Rowan sat on a fallen bough, her ankles deep in the long grass. She picked a blade and chewed it, watching him carefully. 'You've lost your magic disc, too.'

He almost put a hand up to his neck. Without it he

148

felt uneasy. She looked the same, but he knew only too well what she could make him see, and not see.

He came over, and sat beside her.

'Why did you come back?' she asked, almost gently. 'For Mick?'

He pushed the hair from his forehead with both palms, not looking at her. 'In a way.'

'It's too late.'

'Is it?'

'Oh yes. You know what it cost you to break with us. Do you want him to go through all that?'

He didn't answer. Even now, there were places in his memory that he couldn't go; scorching corners of pain that he kept away from.

'I hated you,' he muttered.

She laughed. 'Hatred and love are the same in the end.'

'They're not.'

She slipped down and knelt on the grass in front of him, looking up into his face. 'But they are.'

'How would you know? You can't feel.'

Rowan smiled. 'Now that's not true, and you know it. We just have our own ways. I was very fond of you.'

'You were killing me. Taking everything out of me.'

'That's what music does.' She scratched her cheek, silver bracelets sliding down her arm. 'Our music. And ours is the best. Once you've heard it, all the rest is a jangle of noise. The world is empty without it. That's why you've come back Alex. Isn't it?'

For a long time he couldn't answer, struggling to find words, to keep himself calm, keep out of the darkness that threatened him. When he looked up she was gone, the grasses slowly uncreasing, and he wasn't even sure if she'd ever been there, or whether he had spoken to himself, argued with himself, as he had night after night, time after time, for months.

He went over to the fountain and bent, splashing cold water on his face. Katie was still missing, he told himself, glancing up at the house. A window was open, a round window on the top floor, and for a moment he saw a young fair woman looking out of it. Their eyes met. Then she turned and was gone.

Alex dried his face awkwardly on his sleeve. The pool was a glimmer of reflections, sun-glints, shards of light. He narrowed his eyes against them, and then stared. Something swung there, a shadow, flashing in bright rings, and he looked quickly up to the statue and saw to his amazement that from the god's outstretched hand something swayed, a small circular disc on a chain, spinning in the breeze.

Bewildered, he hauled himself up on the rim of the fountain; took the disc from Apollo's fingers and stared at it.

'How did you get this?' he whispered.

The stone face smiled at him, calm and unseeing.

'Hey! What are you doing up there!'

A thin-haired greying man had come out of the Hall and was hurrying across the lawn, a clipboard under one arm.

Alex jumped down, slipping the chain over his neck. The man came up to him, slightly out of breath. 'What are you doing? You're from the Fair, aren't you?'

Alex nodded. Then he said, 'You're Mick's father.'

Michael Carter looked resigned. 'You know him.'

'We're both musicians.' The breeze blew Alex's hair into his eyes; he brushed it away and said recklessly, 'He's in trouble. You do know that, don't you?'

Mr Carter stared in disbelief. 'What on earth are you talking about?'

'He's unhappy. Unhappy enough to go.'

'Go?'

'Run away. Is music so much to ask for?'

'This is utter rubbish!' Mr Carter sputtered.

'Is it? When did you see him last?'

Mr Carter opened his mouth to retort, then was silent.

'I had no one to help me,' Alex said desperately 'but he's got you. Or he should have. He needs you.'

Mick's father stared at the harper in sudden fury. 'I don't see,' he snarled 'what business this is of yours. My son is my responsibility. And keep off that fountain!'

As he strode away Alex looked after him, fingering the disc. It hadn't worked. It wouldn't, without Katie. Running the familiar smoothness through his fingers, he remembered the changeling's spiteful quip.

Where would they have put her that was underground?

It was definitely a crack.

She scrabbled at it with the broken piece of brick; another chunk of soil fell down. Not a wall, some sort of earth partition made to look like that. Maybe an ice-house, underground tunnels, another cellar. Frantic with hope, Katie rammed the brick into it hard, digging and scratching, willing the faint glow of daylight to strengthen. It had taken ages to find where the light was leaking in; by her watch it was already eight. She was starving and filthy; her face must be smeared with grime. But this had to be a way out!

Soil fell; the hole grew. Beyond it was a paler darkness, a stink of rottenness that made her catch her breath. Doubtful, she stared in. Stories of walled-up bodies came into her head, and she told herself not to be stupid, but it was hard not to think of it, here in the dark.

Something shifted behind her.

She turned, imagining the vast cellars in the dimness. Rats. One was gnawing wood nearby, a relentless scratching. She turned back to the hole, took a breath, and reached her arm inside.

Nothing.

Face and shoulder pressed against the earth wall, she groped in air. Then she came to something soft; a floor, thick with dust and mould. Small wet things scuttled over her fingers. She touched a hardness, rounded and smooth, one end splintered, and her fingers explored it, the forehead's dome, the nose ridge, the concave orbits of lost eyes. She jerked back then, shuddering. She knew a skull when she felt it.

After a second, she made herself try again. Her fingers flexed, she stretched beyond the litter of bones, into emptiness.

When the hand came and held hers it was cold.

And she screamed.

The burial chamber waited for him, even in daylight. It took him all his courage to come out from the trees and stand there, by the mossed stones of the entrance.

No one was around. Unless they were here, he

152

thought, hiding, watching from the high branches.

Alex came forward, slowly.

The wood was still and sultry. No birds sang. The breeze had dropped; nothing moved among the dark green ferns of the clearing, the stiff feathers of the nailed corpses.

He crouched down, and looked inside the barrow.

In all the bad times, in the hospital, in the nightmares and panics and fits of shivering that he'd thought would drive him mad, this had been the place he could never face, never think about. This had been the entrance to all his dreams and ambitions, a place very like this one, miles away, but just the same, leading to the same darkness, the same surrender of his own existence.

'Katie?' he whispered, desperately.

A crow flew up out of the wood, karking. He bent and stooped under the lintel-stone, imagining the weight of it above him, the rammed chalk and deer antlers of its builders.

'Are you here?'

He had no choice. It took all his strength but he went on, stooped, his hands feeling the cold sides of the stone passage, the damp glisten of rainwater, going deeper and deeper into the darkness until he felt it was swallowing him whole, and his breath came ragged, with an effort.

There were side chambers; he groped in each one, feeling only the heaviness and chill of stone, its enclosing presence. He knew he was going too deep, began to panic with the oppression of the earth over him, the tiny remote circle of light that was the way back.

'Katie!'

She had to be here. He knew them; knew their ways. Groping into the last chamber he felt the dim walls with outstretched fingers, praying he would touch her, but the fear was too much for him now, he couldn't bear it, he had to get out, to run, to stop the darkness choking him with its death. Gasping, he crouched, head low, both fists on the floor.

There was a pillar in the chamber, carved with spirals. He slumped against it, shivering, knowing his strength was gone. In the darkness ahead of him something rustled, slid down, crumbled into a hole.

He stared at it. Then, with his last courage, he reached out, into the dark.

Her hand gripped his. It felt so warm, he thought.

The Fair was packed with people. Lammas Day was always the climax, the busiest day. In all the tents, sessions were playing, dancers and musicians crowding the stages. Mick watched a man on stilts stride out of the wood, his great striped trousers fluttering against the poles of his ankles.

'One of yours?'

'They're all mine,' she smiled, coming out to stand at the front of the stall, the silver bracelets sliding down her arms. 'Everything is mine.'

'Even me?'

'Especially you.'

He smiled, breathing a few soft notes into the flute. Then he began to play properly, settling back and closing his eyes, the sun warm on his face.

All night he hadn't been home. All night the music

had gone on, and he could still hear it, all round him. Home was distant and strange; his father and Sandy like shadows. Had he ever really cared about them? He couldn't remember. There had been someone else, but he couldn't remember her, either.

Whistling into a merrier tune he looked up and saw Rowan still watching.

'When do we go?' he asked restlessly.

'When the Ritual ends,' she said. 'At sunset.'

'I just don't understand how I can be here!' Katie stared round at the gloomy trees in utter confusion. 'I was under the Hall. I was in some sort of cellar.' She picked a thread of cobweb off her waist, and thought of the rope.

'You weren't.' He crumpled on a fallen log and rubbed his forehead with a damp hand. 'They made you think that. You can never trust what you see with them.'

She looked back at the burial chamber, its gaping darkness. Then she said, 'It must have been hard, going in.'

He smiled, wan. 'A bit.'

'A lot.' She came over and crouched. 'Are you all right?'

He shrugged. 'I think so.'

'I never thought you'd come back. I can't believe you've found me!'

'I wasn't going to. I suppose I realised I can't run away from myself.'

Katie looked at him. 'You know all about them, don't you?'

He looked down at his hands. 'All about them.' Then he glanced up. 'Look, they don't know you're out. If we can get to Mick . . . what's wrong?'

She was staring past him, out of the wood, at the sky. It was dark, mottled with pale cloud, the moon bright and high.

'Oh god!' she breathed. 'How long were we in there?' Her watch had stopped. She shook it, furiously.

Alex whirled round, he was running, crashing through the still branches and she raced after him, until they burst out on to the lakeshore and saw, to their horror, the blue lightbulbs all along it, hanging in bright festoons.

'It's night! How can it be night!'

'Time goes differently . . .'

'But the sun's gone!' she gasped. 'We have to get back, before the Ritual, before they take Mick!'

Before them, the lake rippled. Harp music rang, soft and subtle, from the Field. Distant thunder rumbled the sultry night.

Behind them, the wood was choked with giggles.

'It's already started,' Alex said.

TWENTY

Old Hag you have Killed me.
TRAD. REEL

Seven great wheels leapt and flamed downhill, fire flaring
off them in streaks and searing arcs. The crowd whooped
and yelled, scattering as the leading one came rolling
wildly into the Lammas Field, slewing over, crashing on
its side, a whole fountain of sparks erupting from it. The
twilight stank of burned wood and charred straw.

As the other wheels collapsed round them the crowd
surged in, lighting torches and flares, and Mick ran with
them, bewildered by the faces round him, small ugly men,
lovely girls, children, men in beast-masks, their eyes and
jaws gleaming in the flamelight – cats, wolves, a bear in a
shaggy cape that capered and lolloped through the
screaming crowd. The Fair people were here somewhere
– he glimpsed Martin briefly, staring at him as if in fear
– but then Rowan came running out of the host, and
caught his elbow. She was wearing a dress of darkest
purple, all dusted with tiny stars.

'Come on!' she whispered. 'It's about to start!'

They hustled him along. He couldn't stop, couldn't
turn round. Far off he thought he heard someone yelling
his name, but the music broke out then and drowned it,
a wild, skirling mixture of reels and strathspeys that set
everyone dancing. All round him torches flared, sparklers,

bits of plaited straw, shimmers of distant lightning, and as he was crowded to the centre of the Lammas Field he saw with a shudder of awe that the Henge had been raised, springing up overnight as it always did, as if by magic.

Twelve great poles they were, of unseasoned wood, smelling of sap and forest, their branches lopped, their barks still crumbling with woodlice and small beetles, and a great lintel all around the top, notched and cut to fit. It was stark and ominous, rearing up in the twilight, a survivor from some lost prehistoric mystery, the protection and sorcery of the harvest. This year things were different; the poles had been carved with faces and strange spirals, cup marks, moon rings, all hung with flowers and plaited shapes of straw – lozenges, cork screws, sunbursts. Sheaves of newly-cut barley were propped against them.

The crowd pressed tight all around the Henge but left its centre empty, a circle of trampled grass with a few daisies like ghost flowers in the purple light.

The night was hot and sultry. Thunder rumbled, far over the fields.

Smoke stung Mick's eyes. He was pushed and shoved through; once he tried to pull back, suddenly uneasy, his heart thudding with a surge of fear, but they forced him to the front, a confusion of sparks and faces and sudden dark. Rowan was waiting. Her face lit when she saw him; she caught hold of his wrist and pulled. 'Come on!' she said, laughing.

He stumbled after her into the empty ring.

Alex shoved his way desperately through the crowd, Katie

struggling behind him, yelling Mick's name. Sparks stung her cheek; she pushed someone's hand away and it was a paw, black-furred, gone before she screeched.

'Keep close to me!' the harper yelled, glancing back.

The disc was powerful. She saw how the tight wedge of bodies divided in front of him, squirming back; caught their hisses and hostile stares, their eerie cold beauty.

Then without warning a troupe of Morris men were all round them, faces all blackened with soot, eyes outlined in red like demons from a nightmare. One of them played a fiddle, the others danced, a furious madcap antic of clashing sticks, their tall hats glossy with pheasant feathers stuck at every angle.

Too fast to stop himself, Alex stumbled against one; instantly the whole dance opened with a hiss, leaving an empty avenue of twilight between its two rows, the music yowling to abrupt silence.

A long roll of thunder echoed. Alex stopped; Katie moved closer. All the soot-black faces watched them curiously.

'Can't keep away, harper,' a voice mocked.

'Walk straight through,' Alex murmured. He was pale, his eyes oddly bright. 'They can't hurt us.'

She wondered if he said it for her, or for himself.

'We can't hurt them!' another voice taunted.

'That's what he thinks.'

'Come and dance, mortal child.' A hand with painted fingers grasped Katie's; she flung it off angrily.

Alex moved; she went with him. They walked through the tense silence of the dance, the soot-faced creatures watching on each side, eyes sharp; some squatting, some leaning on their long white sticks. At the end the Fool stood, blocking the way, a bizarre creature, his face painted half black, half white, his dark hair waist-long and glossy under the feathered hat.

Alex didn't stop. Katie bit her lip. She could sense the dancers closing in behind her, the skin on her shoulders and arms prickling with their closeness and the sultry, electric heat.

The Fool folded his arms. Alex still walked on, till they were almost face to face. At the last minute the faery creature stepped aside and bowed with elaborate, mocking courtesy.

Alex walked straight past him into the crowd. Hot with relief, Katie caught him up: behind them, the whole troupe exploded into laughter.

Now, through smoke and sparks that rose into the night, they could see the Henge. It towered up, lit with a red glow, and shouldering and squeezing through the mass of children and dancers and stiltwalkers Katie finally saw the two creatures she had known she would see, that were there every year, facing each other in the darkness of the ring.

The Corn King was young. He wore a mask with a face like Apollo's, grave and calm, the crown of cornstalks and poppies plaited round his head, his hair straw-coloured, stiff.

Opposite him, in the shadows, stood the Hag. She was shapeless, a mass of corn, wearing a great cape of it right down to her feet, so that she rustled as she moved, like some living sheaf. Her mask was a hooked nose, a gather of hideous wrinkles, but through the eye-holes her eyes were green and watchful.

And in her hand she had the knife, long and sharp.

Alex stopped dead; Katie stumbling into him. She looked round, frantic. 'Where is he?' she gasped.

The harper's hand reached for the disc at his neck.

'Look for the horse,' he yelled.

Sandy sat at the open window.

Out of sight, over in the Field, she heard the furious music of the Lammas, and yet if she concentrated through the hushing of tree-branches, she could make out the crop in the far-away fields, stirring and bending in its long heavy rows, a soft restless movement at the edge of her senses.

For a long time she listened to it, as if it were a voice. When the thunder rumbled it was distant, over the hills.

She stood up and turned, her shadow falling on the bed.

Mick's room was dark, the ceiling a mass of clustered shadows each tinkling its own faint note. They seemed to her all at once to be alive, relentless in their whispering, making soft enticing sounds full of brittle beauty and some sort of longing, a longing she could feel rising in herself as she listened to them, for something she couldn't explain or even imagine. For a moment, she felt reckless with wanting it.

Then Anna gave a small gurgle from the cot next door.

Sandy shuddered.

The chimes clinked in the airless night, sweet and cold.

Suddenly she ran over to the bed, flipped off her shoes and jumped up on it. Working frantically she snatched the wind-chimes down, ignoring the hail of drawing-pins, clutching them tight so they wouldn't

161

tinkle, wouldn't make even a chink of sound ever again. She was amazed at how many there were. When they were all off, she dragged the pillowcase from the pillow and shoved them inside it, stifling them, stuffing them down, muffling them up as if they might cry out.

Breathless, she stepped down on to the carpet. Groping for her shoes, she knew her whole body was trembling, as if after some great race or struggle, but she'd take them down to the bin. She'd finish it.

Bundling the sack under her arm, she paused at the door, looking back.

In the moonlight the room was quiet. Through the twilight, only the tree-stir murmured.

'Katie!'

Michael Carter shouldered through to her, hot and raging. 'For God's sake,' he snarled, 'who are all these people? Someone told me this morning that Mick was . . .' Then he saw Alex.

'You! It was you.'

Katie squirmed round. 'Mick's in trouble.'

'But where is he! I've been looking all day!'

'With Rowan. You know her?'

'I know. But what . . .'

She took a deep breath. 'We think they're going to take him away. With them.'

He stared at her, then at Alex. The fiddling and whistling was rising to a pitch; it roared from the ranks of musicians, the familiar music of the Lammas, but made strange, made dangerous.

The Hag raised her arms, the knife gleaming; the Corn

King watched her through the slits of his mask. She circled, but he stood still in the twilight, the early moon through the trees silvering the edges of the henge.

'Do you mean those travellers are going to abduct my son?'

'He wants to go,' Alex said quietly.

'Rubbish! Where are they?'

'I don't know!' Katie spun round. 'But something's wrong here. The knife is wrong. Look at the knife!'

It was real. They saw that then. Not the blunt wooden replica — more like a scythe, hooked and sharp, the moonlight catching its edge.

The Hag screeched. All the crowd laughed with her, a hiss of glee, and then before Alex could catch hold of her Katie was running out, ignoring the swinging blade, grabbing the Corn King and dragging him back, dragging him away. The crowd hissed and whistled. 'Cut the Corn!' someone shouted, and the cry became a rage of voices, an angry, vengeful stamping. 'Cut the Corn! Cut it down!'

Relentless, Katie held him tight while he struggled. The Hag stood still, her arms folded over the cornstalks. Then Mr Carter was there, bewildered and white. 'What's going on Katie? Tell me!'

'Here!' Too breathless to explain, she grabbed the mask and snatched it away. A jolt of terror shot through her as the lightning glimmered; the boy glared back at her, tousled and gleeful.

She stared at him, tingling with shock.

It wasn't Mick.

TWENTY-ONE

And see ye not that bonny road
Which winds about the fernie brae?
That is the road to fair Elfland
Where you and I this night maun gae.

TRAD.

The crowd roared with laughter.

They rocked and screamed; Katie went hot with fury.

'Where is he!' She shook the boy but he was giggling so much she dropped him in wrath and turned on the Hag.

'Tell me!'

The Hag lowered her mask; an identical wrinkled face was behind it. She gave them a knowing wink.

Katie clenched her hands into fists, but by now Alex had caught her arm; he tugged her out of the henge and out of the crowd, Mr Carter pushing behind, the hoots and jeers loud around them, the music erupting again.

'I know where they'll be,' he yelled.

They ran across the Field. It was deserted; scraps of litter blew in the rising wind; the fires were low, smouldering out. Most stalls were closed, others abandoned; their owners at the Ritual, all the shutters up and the coloured lightbulbs swinging, strangely forlorn. A paper bag gusted against Katie's ankles as she ran. Briefly, she felt the sadness of the Fair's end. Tomorrow everyone would be packing up, going their own ways. It was Lammas, and it was August, the harvest was being cut and though there were warm days ahead, the high point of summer had come and gone; the year had turned, and she felt she had lost something, as she always did.

They raced out of the gate, through the rows of cars, on to the lawns of Stokesey.

Looking up, she saw the moon above the dark glitter of the lake. The house was blank, without lights; there was only the moonlight here, blurred, white-edged, and the silent flicker of lightning. The lawns were silver, and so was the summerhouse, a small pavilion of pale wood. And there at the lake's edge she suddenly saw a white horse, cropping grass, its harness glinting with tiny bells. Rowan was swinging herself up on to its back; then she leaned down for Mick, who was holding the horse's head, stroking it, the flute-case tight under his arm.

He took one look back, and saw them.

He stood very still.

Katie ran up to him and stopped. The coldness in his look repelled her. 'Don't go,' she breathed.

He glared over her shoulder. 'Why bring him? I told you to stay out of it!'

'Don't be stupid. Of course I can't!' She felt Mr Carter loom up behind her, breathless.

'What's going on, Michael?' he said, sounding lost.

Mick glanced up at Rowan. She raised an eyebrow, amused.

Turning back, he said, 'You wouldn't understand. You don't care about me playing, but they do. I've learned from them. I know how to do it now.' He came closer, as if he was trying to bridge some gap. 'I'm not nervous now, not stumbling and scared like I used to be. There's this power inside me. I won't let you take it away.'

His father pushed past Katie. 'Of course we care,' he growled.

'Do you?'

'You know we do.' He glanced up at Rowan. 'Are you filling his head with all this?'

'We gave him what you never could,' she said. 'We're his family now.'

'Rubbish.' Calming himself, he turned to Mick. 'Come home. The Fair's over. I know I've been too busy. Sandy's had Anna but there's been no one for you.'

'It's not that.' Mick looked away, as if he was upset.

'It is. At least that's part of it.'

'No!' He turned and went to the horse.

Quickly Alex said, 'I understand.'

Mick whirled round, wary. 'You! I don't even know you.'

'I know you. And I know her.' He looked up at Rowan; she smiled at him.

'Once you did, Alex.'

'Maybe.' He walked forward and took the flute case from Mick. 'This music,' he said harshly, 'they don't give it to you. It's in you; they just let you find it. And don't make my mistake, don't think they can take it away, because they can't. I've found that out for sure.'

Rowan frowned; she slid down from the horse. 'Take no notice Mick. You're with us.'

Mick looked uneasy; Alex gave a quick glance at Mr Carter, who muttered, 'I can see I've been wrong. I thought it would all wear off, be just a phase, but if it means that much to you, we can arrange things.'

Mick stared at his father in bewilderment. 'Things?'

Mr Carter shrugged, a slight, unhappy movement. 'Lessons. College. Whatever.' He looked at Alex, then back at his son. 'I had a few ambitions when I was younger. The world rolled over them. I shouldn't let that happen to you.'

Rowan watched Mick. 'We should go.'

For a moment he was still; then he turned. His father grabbed him. 'I'm not letting you go!'

'No!' Mick squirmed back.

'Hold him!' Alex was watching Rowan. 'Whatever he does, whatever he says, keep hold of him!'

Icily, she glared at him. 'He's mine,' she hissed.

Mick fought, viciously. 'Let me go! I don't want to stay! I hate Anna and I hate Sandy. Why did you have to bring them here?'

'You don't,' his father murmured.

'I do! It's all gone, all of it! You don't even care!'

He was someone else, bitter, cold, and as Katie watched in horror she almost thought she saw him transform, flicker his shape to hideous, inhuman things, scaly, clawed: a crackle of flame that scorched in the lightning.

'He's mine!' Rowan snarled, but Katie had hold of him too now, and his father grabbed him round the shoulders and clutched him fiercely. 'You're not going,' he kept shouting. 'You're not.'

Mick was sobbing. 'I hate you,' he hissed, but it was weak, and his father said, 'You don't, Mick,' his voice choked, and after that there was silence, except for Mick's breathing, and Katie saw how his hands clutched his father's arms, the flute-case lying unnoticed in the grass.

Rowan was white, quivering with fury. Over Mick's head she watched Mr Carter with narrow eyes.

'This isn't the end of it. You've torn him in pieces!'

Mick looked up.

And then the harper dropped the disc, small and bright, into his fingers.

'Let that help you,' he whispered.

Mick shivered. His face went white in the moonlight, and as he looked at Rowan, he shuddered and cried out. Alarmed, Katie grabbed him again but he didn't notice, staring at the woman in disbelief.

'What is it? What can he see?' Katie muttered.

'Leave him.' Alex sounded harsh, almost cruel. 'He's seeing the truth.'

She was glad she couldn't see it. Mick looked sick; he stumbled back against his father, who put his arm round him and held him.

Alex watched. 'You can never trust them,' he said bitterly. 'All you see is illusion. You don't ever know how they feel, because what they feel isn't love.' He looked up, and she shrugged her slim shoulders at him.

'Sometimes,' he whispered, 'I'm not sure if they even exist.'

Rowan shrugged. 'We exist.' She looked at Mick. 'Don't we.'

Mick was bewildered. He felt so strange, as if he was coming back to himself after some long fever, and it had begun out here, in the summerhouse, with one sound, one exquisite chime of notes. He felt he had been rooted to this spot ever since, in some charmed sleep, listening.

She was a stranger to him now. He had never really known her, this woman with her green, mocking eyes.

Cold with fury, Rowan swung herself up, gathered the silver reins in her hands, so the horse stepped back.

'Have it your way, Mick. If you ever call, I might come back. But all your life, through all the years and months, and illnesses and sorrows, you'll hear my Branch. Even when you're an old man, you'll hear it. And you'll wish for me then. Because we don't grow old.'

He didn't want to hear. He turned to his father. 'I'm sorry,' he muttered. 'I'm really sorry.'

'Not you, Mick. Me.' Mr Carter looked up at Rowan. 'Growing old isn't so bad, with people you love around you.'

She nodded, gravely. 'It's a lie I've heard before.'

The horse circled them, her dress rustling on its back, her cropped hair dark. The tiny moons glinted from her ears. 'You won't forget, Mick. Ask him.'

Her green eyes turned to Alex; he stood still and silent, watching her. For a second their eyes met; she nodded as if she understood him. Then she turned the horse away.

It stepped daintily over the grass to the water's edge. And there it walked out on to the rippling lake, over the small waves, the bells on its harness chinking, out into a chill mist that had risen. Deeper and deeper the horse walked into it, until it was a shadow and a grey ghost, and then it was gone, and she had never once looked back.

They stood there, listening, the lake water lapping in faint ripples against their feet.

Walking back over the lawns, no-one said much. Thunder came faint, far over the cornfields. Mick walked with his father; Katie followed with Alex. Coming past the statue of Apollo she glanced up at it. The grave smile of the young god was wan in the moonlight.

Mick managed a smile. 'Thanks, Katie,' he said.

She pushed the orange tangle from her face. 'I didn't do much. Alex did.'

He and Mick looked at each other. Abruptly Mick burst out, 'It was true, wasn't it? About not losing the music? I won't feel I'll never be as good as I might have been?'

Alex was silent. When he answered his voice was steady.

'It was true.' He touched the disc in Mick's hand. 'Keep that. In case you ever think you dreamed her.'

Suddenly, right in front of them, the main door of Stokesey was unbolted with a startling crack of sound; a great slot of light swivelled out and dazzled them, and they saw Sandy waiting at the top of the steps.

'So here you all are!' she said. 'Is it over? Are we going to this concert?'

Mick's father grinned. 'I suppose so,' he said. 'It's about time I heard my son play.'

He went up the steps to her; Mick stared at his back, then turned to Katie, pale as a ghost.

'Did he say that?'

She smiled. 'He did.'

'Can I see you later?'

'Oh yes,' she said fervently. 'I want to hear all about this. I've got a few things to tell you.'

He looked back at the lake. 'I suppose I should be

glad. But I don't. I just feel . . . empty.'

She knew that. Somehow she felt it herself.

But then the harper pushed the flute-case into his hands, and he opened it, almost shy.

In the moonlight the silver pieces of the flute were warm and smooth.

Alex walked Katie to the Field. 'I'll be gone by tomorrow,' he said quietly, at the gate.

Katie nodded. 'We'll see you in Scotland? At Glastonbury? You should get a few bookings now.'

He looked down, rubbing his lank hair with one hand. 'I'll always owe you a debt Katie, for getting me to play that night. I won't forget that.'

She laughed it off, awkward. Music came from the main marquee, a warm, merry reel.

'Goodbye, Katie,' he muttered.

She watched him walk into the twilight; then turned, heading for home. It was dark now, and from the Henge the smoke drifted, a smell of sausages sizzling on the air. The Ritual must have gone on; tomorrow the corn would be cut on all the fields of Stokesey.

She never knew what made her turn so sharply.

Alex was a shadow by now, between the shuttered stalls. Suddenly, her heart thumping, she found she was running after him, keeping out of sight behind canvas shelters, the closed and silent ice-cream van.

He was walking through the Fair. No one was around. No one saw her. But under the shadows of the trees there was movement, a clink of sound so sweet it stopped Katie in shock, all her skin crawling. She crouched down, her hands tight on the tentpole of an empty stall.

171

The horse was waiting, white and tall. The woman on it was Rowan, and yet not her, a woman with a gypsy tangle of black hair, a wide gold crescent gleaming at her neck. In one hand she carried a silver branch; with the other she reached down to him. He jumped up on a bench and swung himself up behind her, the horse circling restlessly.

They spoke, but Katie was too far to hear it. The woman brushed his hair and he laughed, a low sound, full of relief.

Then they turned the horse and walked it into the wood, its hooves soft in the muffling leaves.

She never knew how long she crouched there. All she knew was the darkness and the distant reels and clapping, and that her eyes were wet, her fingers picking rough shavings off the pole.

Behind her, the smoke of the Lammas fires drifted over the Field.